The Owl with the Golden Heart

Simon Cowell

Printed and Published in the UK
by TAW, Brookfield Cottage,
Bickington Road, Bickington,
Barnstaple, Devon EX31 2NA, UK

Set in Palatino 11pt

2 4 6 8 10 12 14 16 18

ISBN: 978-0-9567753-0-6

In 2009, Lou and Simon Cowell published their first book – *Wildlife SOS*. Subtitled *True stories from Britain's favourite animal rescue centre*, this popular paperback provided a glimpse into the world of Simon's Surrey-based animal rescue centre – introducing us along the way to many remarkable animal characters.

Now, Simon has brought to life a story which he first began writing some 20 years ago… In its chapters we meet One-Eye – an owl who has found himself suddenly transported from the wild to the intensive care unit at the Wildlife Aid centre. One-Eye is puzzled and frightened – torn from his natural realm by injury and the careless indifference of man. Sadly, One-Eye is not alone, and he soon finds himself sharing his misfortune and misery with a variety of creatures from Britain's endangered and shrinking countryside.

This is no ordinary animal story: this is a book which attempts to understand the feelings of animals – to explore and imagine what they might be thinking, what they might be saying to each other, and, more importantly, what they might be saying to human beings if only they could talk to us. The impetus for this book stems from the passionate vision of Simon Cowell and his dedicated colleagues at Wildlife Aid, as they fight to redress the balance between Man and Nature, and to care for and nurse Britain's beautiful wild creatures – the heritage which should belong to us all.

Dedications...

In this, our first 30 years of Wildlife Aid, there have been simply too many people who deserve a special dedication. But I am going to be brave and put names to a few of the very important individuals who have been so instrumental to our success.

Firstly, this book is dedicated to my father – tutor, mentor, friend. I miss his inspiration and presence every single day. Perhaps without him, Wildlife Aid would never have come into being.

Secondly, a dedication to Jill who single-handedly ran Wildlife Aid for the first 14 years – taking it from an earnest hobby to the status of a real, serious wildlife rehabilitation centre. Thirdly, a huge thank-you to Penny Stansil, who painstakingly typed up the manuscript for this book – starting by deciphering my illegible scribble!

Finally, to my daughters, Louisa and Gemma, who have known no normal "privacy" or family life! From their earliest years, they often came down to breakfast – tripping over hedgehogs, or ducking as owls swooped across the kitchen. I would also like to apologise to them if I was ever too wrapped up in my work – collecting an injured fox, looking after a new patient in the hedgehog wing – to read to them, or help with homework.

Simon Cowell, MBE
Leatherhead, Surrey, October 2010

Foreword
By Julie Walters CBE

Another book of animal stories? *No!* At least, not an ordinary story of living with or caring for animals, but a book all about the world of wild creatures, not far from our own backdoor, and their treatment at the hands of humans – all seen from the point of view of the owl, magpie, fox and hedgehog who find themselves in the care of "Two Legs" – Simon Cowell, the founder of Wildlife Aid.

If animals could talk, what you will read in this book is what they would say! Puzzled by the injuries that have befallen them, they do at least find some nice, compassionate human beings to nurse them back to health. And what a place Wildlife Aid is! An independent rescue-centre, sanctuary, hospital and 'drop-in' for all sorts of winged, four-legged, or even two-legged creatures. What would we do without it? And what would *animals* do without the caring, dedicated volunteers who give them the chance to heal, recuperate – and live?

This is a book you must read – that *we must all read!* It is about the pain that injured animals feel, the injustice that they encounter, and the fantastic work of one man and his small charity in Surrey that, on a daily basis, is "actively caring for British wildlife".

Introduction

*"Love the animals. God has given them the
rudiments of thought and joy untroubled.
Don't trouble it, don't harass them,
don't deprive them of their happiness,
don't work against God's intent."*

Dostoyevsky

"An odd feeling entered his mind, as a partial
consciousness infused his rigid body, and, with it, a
sense of foreboding also began to emerge, without a
distinct form. He was lying down. But owls don't lie
down! Why then had he adopted this most unnatural
position? Perhaps he had died after all and there was
no Great Tree Owl, no greater glory…"

A life changed, the torment, pain and strangeness of
not knowing what has happened to you – and why
you can no longer fly, or crawl or run free… These are
the stories of One-Eye, an injured owl, and his many
friends – Crow, Fox, Woody, Old Prickle and Magpie
– who find themselves in the care of a human being
who loves Nature.

The world of these beautiful animals is set with traps
and danger, which no animal – programmed as they
are by God-given instinct and the rudiments of

thought – could ever anticipate. It falls to the moral impetus of Two Legs to do what is right, to nurse the animals back to health and to rage against those who have sought to destroy their free-running spirits.

At Wildlife Aid, each animal is treated as a character – a person in their own right. And it is the empathy with wild creatures which brings these fascinating individual stories to life – taking us closer to an animal's-eye view of the world, and nearer to the vision of the charity that does so much to restore the imbalance between Man and Nature.

The Owl with the Golden Heart

Chapter 1

One-Eye's Story

As One-Eye flew continuously over his usual hunting grounds in the blustery wind, he was reminded of the terrible night, many seasons ago, when an unyielding storm had thrown him into a nearby tree. It was in that instant he had lost his eye, plucked from him by a protruding twig. Now, as his three-foot wingspan carried him across the dark fields, over low hedgerows and amidst the sparse trees of his childhood, he flew with extra caution, because his one eye was his total lifeline.

Quartering the nearly pitch-black field again and again, searching out a meal for his family, One-Eye was aware of just how lucky he'd been to have adapted and survived with his limited hunting ability. Gone, was his superb

perception of distance and his virtually complete success rate where it came to seizing his prey (nature can be cruel) and he thanked the Great Tree Owl that he had been fortunate enough to make it through those first, critical days after his accident – the pain, the lack of balance.

Many of One-Eye's old friends had been taken in that cruel night, many homes destroyed and there was, for months afterwards, a palpable note of fear and horror in the air, as all the local residents desperately tried to create new homes before the winter firmly set in.

Tonight, as the chilling currents rippled through his feathers, One-Eye felt uneasy; something in him sensed the very same vibrations in the air now, as had been present on that terrible night. His still finely acute hearing was picking up strange noises from far away and, as the moon vanished behind a sea of vast black clouds, he was forced to hunt nearer the ground. This way, he could make use of the more unrestricted areas where he would have a better chance of seeing, or sensing, a likely supper.

As the minutes passed, One-Eye couldn't help but notice his flight becoming more erratic; his powerful primary feathers had to keep twisting and angling to cope with the increasing wind. He was always nervous in these conditions. If he had not had to find food for his family, he would happily have foregone his meal for the safety of his home and the happy calling of his nearby relations.

Just as he crossed over a low hedgerow he sensed, rather than saw, movement in the sparse undergrowth below and, instinctively, swooped down, to give his one good eye a chance of confirming these suspicions. This was not his preferred hunting ground, owing to the danger of the Lightning Thunder that used these barren, sterile places. Once again, however, he sensed a movement and positioned himself for a final attack. Angling his wings precisely, he targeted his quarry. Then, nothing. Only an instantaneous flash of blinding light and searing pain.

Over the next few hours, One-Eye drifted in and out of consciousness, his mind flicking vaguely between odd snatched scenes of memory. The dark night. The storm brewing. His body hurtling into the front of a Lightning Thunder. A massive pain that stole his breath away. And, all the while, the underlying feeling that it would very soon be his time to perch alongside the Great Tree Owl, as promised in the story handed down through generations; the ultimate glory.

The ache that filled his broken form prevented him from moving; every tiny stir of the breeze grated his torn little body, each passing sound jangled his raw nerves. So he slumped back in acceptance of his fateful journey, ready to join his long-lost friends, those claimed by the previous winter's storm. He just longed for the torment to go away. Why did it have to hurt so much?

One-Eye didn't know where he was. He sensed that he was no longer outside, but had no recollection of anything since being jerked from the skies by the roaring Lightning Thunder. In this place though, there seemed to be no natural refuge to crawl into, to hide away. Whenever he did manage to summon a small amount of energy, he would immediately lose his balance on the unfamiliar, hard, unyielding, flat surface of this strange new environment. There were unusual noises in the far distance and scents and sensations all around him which seemed entirely alien. Drifting in and out of sleep, he was completely unaware of time as it passed and, still, his physical agony consumed him. When he awoke with the taste of blood in the back of his mouth, he knew that it must indeed mean the end was near.

More noise. Then stillness. Followed by footsteps. A soft breath of cold air. And then, in spite of his confused, disorientated state, One-Eye was certain he was in the presence of a Two Legs. He'd seen Two Legs in the past, but never approached them, ever in his life. He was not particularly afraid of them because, unlike many other creatures, they had never done him harm. But he felt uneasy now, as the Two Legs picked him up and he felt his body being gently turned, his legs stretched and his wings minutely examined. This inspection seemed to last for a long time. Then there was a sharp, brief pain in his leg, followed by a deep, blissful sleep. One-Eye prepared to meet the Great Tree Owl, as he closed his eyes.

Chapter 2

The Dream

Time meant little. Nothing filled his brain but dreams; some instantly forgotten, others that kept recurring. Several times he saw an intense light, silhouetting the Great Tree Owl and heard the vague echoes of a deep, resonant voice. Slowly, each time the dream replayed, more and more pieces of the picture began to take definite form in his mind.

The voice, soothingly but firmly, was assuring him that the time was not yet right for his final journey. Saying that, instead, a great honour was to be bestowed upon him and he was not to be afraid. Finally, the jigsaw was complete and the whole – if not yet fully understood – picture, was revealed.

"Oh brave One-Eye, I have observed you over many seasons. I watched your birth and childhood. I saw the understanding and tolerance you showed your kind and I marvelled at the compassion – compassion way beyond your years – which you had for all life around you.

I have watched also, your path into adulthood and the firm, but loving way you have raised your children. I grieved over your accident, but before I could be sure that you were The One, I needed to fulfil this quest; I had to give you one last test. A challenge which would have felled many, but one to which I felt sure you would rise. And rise you have. When I took one of your eyes, you did not falter. You handled the obstacle I put in your path with sureness and dignity. You adapted without fuss and with a stalwart heart which bore no resentment.

Though I have once more given you pain, this is the final pain. Be not afraid of the future, believe in me and I shall guide you to glory. You will have the power to bless others with both acceptance and hope. You will acquire fame among many and your strength and devotion will give you great peace of mind.

Remember, be not afraid of the future, of things unknown to you, and retain your faith in me. For only with your belief can I truly guide you on this epic journey that is your destiny. Accept your new role stoically and, together, we can reach so many. Know that sight is only ever truly in the mind. Be guided by the truth of love and the innate empathy of your fellow beings. I am with you and will fly beside you, always."

The words faded. But over much time One-Eye's dream was to repeat itself over and over, interspaced only by the intermittent, short, sharp pain to his leg.

Chapter 3

The Awakening

An odd feeling entered his mind, as a partial consciousness infused his rigid body, and, with it, a sense of foreboding also began to emerge, without a distinct form.

He was lying down. But owls don't lie down! Why then had he adopted this most unnatural position? Perhaps he had died after all and there was no Great Tree Owl, no greater glory. And if he was lying down, surely, as everyone knew the ground was cold, why did he feel warmth?

His limbs felt so stiff – it was as if he was paralysed, yet he could sense the tips of his wings and the points of his talons, and he felt hungry! A sure sign that he was still alive! Now and then, in his mind, One-Eye's dream drifted back and forth filtering through his pain; "Have faith... don't be afraid... fly beside you..."

All was completely dark too. Before, not even on the blackest of nights, had he been unable make out the basic outlines of nearby shapes and buildings. Terror gripped at his empty stomach and began, again to pervade his useless, unmoving body; "...have faith... ...trust..."

Noise, distant, but definitely there and getting closer. His pain temporarily numbed by panic, One-Eye's remaining senses, minus his sight, were on full alert. The noise, growing nearer by the second, seemed unfamiliar yet, at the same time, not so. Sounds he'd heard as he'd passed in and out of his recent sleep, perhaps? The terror he expected to surge through his body seemed to fade away before it ever really started, and he wanted – wondered – unmoving, unsure.

The collection of sounds now became so close it seemed to surround him. Suddenly he felt his body being picked up and handled and, finally, he recognised the voices of the Two Legs. But, amazingly, everything was still in absolute blackness. Never before had he known these creatures to move around in total darkness. His legs and wings were, once again, very gently manipulated and, following this, he was most surprised to feel his beak and jaw being carefully prised open. He tried to open his beak himself to protest, but strangely found that he had no control over the necessary muscles to do so. The Two Legs spoke to him in tones that were quiet, soothing and, curiously even; reassuring.

He lay, unable to move in their control, waiting for their next move. His beak, again, was forced open and something thrust firmly, deep into his throat. Food! And it was food he recognised. Bliss! He gulped it down and hoped for more, which soon followed and was enough to satisfy his appetite. All this in pitch blackness, though. How very peculiar, thought One-Eye. After his tasty snack, he was gently placed back on the warm surface he'd vacated just a short while before and left in peace. At least, now his hunger had been quenched, he would be able to think more clearly, not only about his strange, recurring dreams, but also of his future.

Why couldn't he move on his own? He worried that his body may be paralysed. Why couldn't he cry out for help? He couldn't even call out to alert others of his presence. Summoning all the energy he could muster from his worn body and concentrating with every grain of willpower he possessed, One-Eye attempted to move, one at a time, each and every muscle in his body. Although there was no longer the sharp intolerable pain, which had consumed him initially, a low, dull ache remained, as though he had flown continuously for many nights without reprieve and was now suffering complete exhaustion.

With each attempt on his wasted muscles, very slowly, he began to flex his legs and wings, inch by inch, until finally he could shuffle into a more dignified sitting position. That was much better! One-Eye felt very proud of himself for managing to at least be upright again, though his efforts had clean worn him out and as he dozed in the warmth of the place he was in, once more the dreams found him.

The voice spoke quietly to him, in congratulatory tones, "Once again brave One-Eye, you have met your challenge with courage and wisdom. You now have the inner strength to begin your new life and do great good; deeds that will, in time, become known throughout our kingdom…"

Roused by an awareness of something being near, the approaching sound of the Two Legs' footsteps alerted all his innate primeval fears. But wait, there was something else. Was it food he could detect? Yes, he was sure it was. Before he knew it, his beak was struggling to open, to gape, like an owlet responding to its mother's call. The shame of it. What was he thinking? Thank goodness everywhere was dark! As he waited for his dinner to be thrust into his mouth, One-Eye began to realise that this time it was different. He felt the food near his beak, gently being moved from side to side; exciting his taste buds, but why wasn't it actually being given to him? He needed it now!

Again the Two Legs' calm, soothing voices were encouraging him from the darkness, so, with great effort, he tried to take the food for himself. It was no use, despite conjuring tempting thoughts of mousy morsels; his beak would not move. Again he tried, and again. Then, slowly, very slowly he managed, through sheer willpower, to open his beak. Just a fraction at first and then a fraction more. But it was no good; he would never have the strength to pick up a meal for himself. The soft voices continued and at the same time he felt his beak being gently opened, helping it to become wide enough to receive the succulent food. At last the reward arrived and One-Eye felt the sumptuous meal being eased into his mouth and down his throat.

Chapter 4

The New Life

Over the next weeks, the days became routine. One-Eye, now fully tolerant of the Two Legs with their warm, soothing voices, grew to realise that they not only meant him no harm, but that, really, they were trying to help him. During this time, he had managed to open his beak a little wider at each feeding and, eventually, with the food always being put in the same place, he started to help himself as and when he fancied a few mouthfuls. He was still puzzled by the prevailing darkness, but each time he roosted and dozed, the Great One's words filtered into his mind, "…Sight is only ever truly in the mind…"

Life, as one long night, was becoming very boring. So One-Eye had set himself a regular regime of exercising every muscle in his body, as much as possible, in the darkness of his new home. "Home," he thought, "funny that I should think of it as home."

His sleep was now more restful and, despite the odd nightmare, which was always calmed by thoughts of the Great One; all seemed well. It was during one particular afternoon nap, some little while later, when he again sensed the glorious light and warmth surround him. He knew, then, that he was about to hear more from his protector.

And so the voice started... "Since your final pain you have done well. You are now ready to embark upon the task for which I have prepared you. Remember, follow your heart, use your wisdom and have faith. Never again will you see outwards, so you must look inwards, into your heart. You will not only begin to see more clearly, but you will come to be of great service to others."

The dream faded and even before he had shaken off his sleep, he heard the Two Legs arrive. There was much commotion; he sensed worry in the air, along with another sensation that he couldn't quite yet place.

All creatures have an extra sense that is there if they care to really try to use it. Owls, particularly, have developed this more than most.

One-Eye knew that sound – the scuffling, the sniffing – a hedgehog, not one of his natural enemies in real life. He felt the creature's fear. He wondered what to do for the best and decided that he would, very quietly, start to call out to the hedgehog. A call which, in his natural woodland, signalled to others that there was no present danger, that all was well.

When the Two Legs eventually left and One-Eye found himself alone with his new companion, "Hey, you," he called softly.

The hedgehog had started to cry quietly.

"Don't be afraid," said One-Eye.

The hedgehog shuffled around and very haltingly asked how he could be so sure. "Why are you here? What happened?" asked One-Eye.

"I was minding my own business," sniffed the hedgehog, "when I smelt a beautiful piece of meat down at the end of a short tunnel. So in I walked and then found that I couldn't move either in or out. I was stuck fast with something sharp cutting into my belly, making me bleed all over the place. The more I struggled, the more I was cut and, still, I could not free myself. I really thought I was going to die."

The hedgehog drew a long shuddering breath and continued.

"I was there for hours, until along came this massive barking dog and picked me up, only to dump me in front of a Two Legs. The tunnel was pulled apart and the Two Legs picked me up, rubbed some foul smelling stuff along my wound and then brought me here."

"Did it hurt much?" asked One-Eye.

"Well, I must admit it was done quite gently, now I think about it," said the hedgehog, "and they kept making funny noises to me. But, my belly still hurts, I'm very hungry and

I want to go home!" The frightened hedgehog then began to cry all over again.

"Don't be afraid," said One-Eye, "It really is not as bad as you might think."

And, with that, he started talking quietly of times gone by, telling old stories that circulated around the woodland. At last the crying slowed and was replaced by a gentle snoring sound.

Time passed and the hedgehog did not wake again until the Two Legs appeared, startling her from her slumber. The crying started immediately, all over again, until she smelt food. The last time that particular scent had stirred her appetite had resulted in her being imprisoned in the tunnel. However, the succulent aroma was altogether too much for her to bear and she scrabbled forward to investigate its source. 'Just one lick,' she thought as she edged closer, making absolutely sure there was no tunnel in sight. Hedgehog's crying turned into a whimper, which, in turn, changed into the noisy slapping of lips, punctuated by general chomping sounds.

One-Eye smiled to himself – food for him too, he thought, and picked up a couple of juicy morsels from his own bowl. The sound of munching was cut short by a very loud burp. "Sorry," said Hedgehog, "I couldn't resist the temptation any longer."

"Don't worry," said One-Eye, "you'll find mealtimes are regular here, no searching for food and disappointment at finding none".

"Burp" went Hedgehog again! "Sorry ..." And with that promptly fell asleep.

Chapter 5

The Community Grows

The owl and the hedgehog found each other to be very good company, as they swapped stories of their past lives.

Feeding times came and went and after every few meals, Hedgehog became accustomed to being picked up by the Two Legs to have her wound bathed. Slowly, she began to feel better. But, the better she felt, the more her need for freedom intensified.

"I don't like this cage," she said to One-Eye, following an afternoon's meal and wound bathing. She started pacing up and down.

"What cage?" asked One-Eye.

"This one," said Hedgehog, who was now pushing her nose up against the mesh door of her enclosure, trying to find an opening.

"...But how can you see in this darkness?" said One-Eye.

"Don't be stupid," said Hedgehog, "it's quite bright in here with the sun shining through the window."

One-Eye remained silent, not panicking, but reflecting quietly on his recent dreams.

Suddenly he realised that the words spoken to him as he slept, were to prepare him for his blindness. All this time, while he'd been recovering from his injuries, it wasn't the whole world that had been cloaked in darkness, just his world. His new world. One-Eye was now completely blind.

With this fresh realisation dawning upon him, One-Eye pondered the situation, and, looking inward, was surprised to find nothing but peace in his heart. The Great One had prepared him well.

Just then, before he could think too much more about his new predicament, there came an ear-piercing screaming noise from out of nowhere, and it was getting closer. The Two Legs approached with what was obviously a terribly frightened animal, struggling to escape from its arms.

One-Eye's door was opened and he was gently lifted out, whilst the thrashing creature was carefully released in his place. One-Eye now called out anxiously, not understanding what was happening.

Hedgehog replied: "It's alright, don't panic, I can see that you're being moved to a much larger space across the room.

Looks luxurious to me, compared to this old box I'm in."

One-Eye, totally unfamiliar with his new surroundings, stayed routed to the spot, too scared to move. But just as he began to quake with fear, the ever-calming voice from his dreams filtered into his mind, "...No time to fear... more work to do... you will be fine… Haven't I said many times that you have felt the final pain and that all will be well? – Help those whom I have entrusted to your care..."

With that, the awful screaming and thrashing started again and the hedgehog, not being terribly brave, immediately curled into a tight ball and went to sleep. So, once again, One-Eye started calling quietly but continuously, from his new enclosure.

"Help!" cried the terrified bird, "Get me out, someone!"

"*Shhhhh*," hushed One-Eye, "are you hurt?"

"Not 'alf" said the screeching newcomer. "There I was, sittin' on the grass, just borrowin' some of the local cat's lunch, when 'e crept up from be'ind, grabbed me wing and rolled me onto me back! Ready to 'ave me as 'is substitute lunch, I shouldn't wonder! I wriggled free, but 'e pounced again and 'eld on firmly to me tail, which 'e then promptly pulled out. I managed to escape, but couldn't fly. Me wing seems to be hangin' at a funny angle – it just won't work at all. As I ran for cover, 'e followed, but a Two Legs saw and scooped me up, put me in a Lightning Thunder and brought me 'ere. Now I'm trapped, I can't get out! 'ELP!"

"Oh, do stop panicking," said One-Eye, who was by now losing his patience with the terrible squawking of the blatantly belligerent crow.

19

Again the Two Legs appeared and, judging by the crow's increased noise level, had obviously picked him up and was examining his injuries.

"'Ger off!" squawked Crow, whilst flapping around trying to find a beakful of something to bite. "Got it!" he yelled in a satisfied manner, expecting the hand to be rapidly withdrawn. But, surprisingly, there was no hasty movement. Instead, his beak was gently opened, it's content released, and the examination continued. "Oh cor blimey!" he squawked, "I'm a goner now."

"Don't be silly," said One-Eye, "you just told us that it was only your wing that doesn't work. These Two Legs will make it right."

"Oh yeah?" said Crow. "Says who?"

"Says me," piped up Hedgehog, who had been awakened from her slumber by the general hubbub.

"Who're you?" asked Crow, still very unsure.

"Just listen," said Hedgehog. "I came in here with a very bad cut across my tummy and now I'm nearly well. I haven't even had to search for food because it was brought to me."

Crow, though not wholly placated, was beginning to lose a little of his initial panic. He felt his wing being moved and then pushed firmly back against his body. The Two Legs wrapped sticky tape all around it – now it wouldn't move at all! "See...see..." he squawked "Now I'm done for – it won't move at all."

"Oh Crow," said One-Eye, becoming cross with his

whining, "it takes time to mend, it's not immediate, just relax and wait."

The Two Legs returned Crow to his cage and just as he was about to start screaming again, a wonderful smell came wafting under his beak from the other side of his enclosure, distracting him from his would-be complaints. He waddled over to investigate.

"Cor blimey," he uttered, "look at this lot, it must be me birthday!" There before him was an array of food that quite took his breath away – even so, before he approached it he carefully glanced around to see that there were no cats close by. Gulp, gulp down went the food, so fast that Hedgehog was amazed. "Burp," went Crow.

"Oh no," said One-Eye, "not two of you with such awful manners!"

"Sorry," said Hedgehog on Crow's behalf.

Chapter 6

The Orphans Flood In

The three patients found that they got on rather well together, despite their differences. Both Hedgehog and Crow understood that One-Eye could not see and took it in turns to help him explore his new home. One-Eye would cautiously edge his way along the boundaries of his pen and the other two would tell him when he came towards a wall or an obstruction.

One-Eye still longed to fly again, but it wasn't until Crow one day squawked up, "…Why ain't you flyin' mate?" that One-Eye actually realised he had enough space to exercise his wings to such an extent.

"I might hit something," he replied.

"So?" said Crow, "You'll only be flyin' slow and we can warn you when you're in danger."

So One-Eye very hesitantly began to beat his wings. For the first time in many weeks, felt himself lift free of the ground.

"Up," said Crow. "One more body length."

"Forward a bit."

"Perch beneath."

One-Eye followed the instructions, stalled his flight and found… nothing. 'Thud!' he fell the short distance right into his food bowl.

"Whoops," said Hedgehog, and Crow sniggered.

"Shh," muttered Hedgehog, "don't make him feel bad." "But 'e's got 'is lunch all over 'is 'ead!"

One-Eye struggled up and cleaned himself off, and, in a very sad manner, stated that it was no good, he wouldn't try again.

"Nonsense!" said Crow, "You nearly 'ad it right, just got to adopt a different technique that's all. You just 'ave to keep 'overing 'til ya feet find the surface. Go on, try again!" So One-Eye did.

"Up."

"Forward."

"Now, just in front of ya is a branch," said Crow. "Forward a bit…"

One-Eye gently hovered and, sure enough, his talons felt and gripped the perch beneath. He was safe! Trying not to show it, but obviously very pleased with himself, One-Eye decided to have a celebratory preen.

"See, easy peasy!" said Crow.

"Well," said One-Eye, "not bad I suppose"

"Just do it slow," said Crow "until you can remember where everything is and then you'll 'ave no trouble."

So One-Eye practised whilst Crow and Hedgehog gave the odd direction or warning. It didn't take long for him to find he was able to fly around very adequately indeed, and he certainly enjoyed the exercise and freedom.

Just as the three friends were settling into a comfortable routine, so the onslaught began.

One morning, long before Hedgehog had woken, the Two Legs came into the hospital with a large, very noisy box. Only this was not the usual sound of injury or pain, but that of tiny babies all crying for food. The inmates watched on as the youngsters were carefully placed in a small cage with a light that kept them warm.

As the Two Legs prepared a special feast for the new arrivals, "Cor, look at that," said Crow. "Wish I could 'ave some of that for lunch."

Very carefully, using a pair of tweezers, the Two Legs fed each baby until their beaks stopped opening and sleep overcame them … Peace … "Thank gawd for that." said Crow, who had watched the feeding intently, "But I really would've loved some of that nosh." And, just as if the Two Legs had understood him, a tweezer full of food was

pushed towards Crow. He wagged his beak, "I'm not eating off them, I ain't no baby."

Still, Crow regretted missing out on the tasty morsel. To his disbelief, despite his initial refusal, the food was proffered again. This time he looked around to check that neither One-Eye nor Hedgehog was watching, and as they weren't, he gulped down the delicious mixture that reminded him so deliciously of his childhood. "Yumm-ee," he thought.

The quietness did not last long. Not only were the babies hungry again, but yet another box arrived, this time with very young squirrels mewing from inside. One-Eye sat thinking that this was where his work really began.

In addition to reassuring frightened adults, he'd also to help the young, to prepare them as best he could for life out in the wild, the life that awaited them just as soon as they were old enough to be released.

Over the next hours there was little peace, with both the young birds and the orphaned squirrels crying, feeding and sleeping at staggered intervals. All three adults were very much looking forward to a good night's sleep as they had not managed to have any short snoozes during the day.

Eventually, One-Eye sensed darkness coming and Hedgehog confirmed his feeling. Yet, unbelievably, still the feeding continued. It seemed very late indeed when, well into the night, finally activity in the shed ceased. The three friends bid each other an exhausted good night, Hedgehog scuffled out for her usual pre-bedtime snack and then all was, at last, silent. Even Crow controlled his usual evening burp.

Chapter 7

Lullaby

One-Eye was woken by the sound of soft but persistent crying. The squirrels were whimpering quietly, obviously feeling thoroughly miserable. "Little ones," called One-Eye in his most soothing voice, "be calm and I shall sing you a song. Snuggle up together in the warmth and listen." Being inquisitive young souls, with, as yet, no fear of owls, the squirrels did as they were told. One-Eye began his melody. In velvety tones he sang to them a lullaby that told of summer days and green trees and all their woodland friends.

Little did One-Eye realise that Hedgehog and Crow had both woken and were also enjoying his midnight song. After a while the shed fell quiet once more, but it seemed a very short night indeed when, just as dawn broke, both the fledglings and the squirrels immediately started up their own "Where's Breakfast?" chorus.

"Fat chance!" thought Crow, cranky from a lack of sleep, "Two Legs are never up this early." So, quite astounded was he when only a few minutes later they appeared with food and milk. Feeding began again in earnest as the three friends looked on. With the babies' food being passed back and forward in front of him, a still half-asleep Crow forgot himself and gaped like a baby. "Fool," he thought to himself, instantly ashamed. But, as it had done the day before, a tweezerful of food suddenly appeared through the bars of his cage and he delightedly gulped it down. It wasn't until Hedgehog said "Baby!" that Crow realised he had been seen and he fluffed out his feathers in embarrassment.

The daytime was harder for the youngsters because they missed the regular to-ing and fro-ing of their parents; the feeding, the cleaning and the stories that they were told. So One-Eye and Hedgehog took it in turns to sing them songs from the woodlands, which kept them reasonably calm between meals. Crow, on the other hand, said it was much too babyish to sing songs and spent the time stomping around his cage, wishing he could fly again. Feeding times came and went and both One-Eye and Hedgehog were exhausted by nightfall.

They all hoped for a better night's sleep, especially Crow who said he'd 'sort out' anyone who made a fuss. Blissfully, as darkness took over, there was not a sound in the shed except that of its peacefully snoring residents. However, just before dawn approached, Crow was awakened by the gentle sobs of one of the baby squirrels; "Where's my Mummy –

where has she gone?" The same phrase repeated many times. Crow coughed, hoping to wake either One-Eye or Hedgehog, who would surely sing the little one back to sleep. Nothing. He coughed again, louder this time, but, alas, the sobbing continued and still no one else woke.

Crow peered through his cage and sure enough both One-Eye and Hedgehog slept on, oblivious. "Tired," thought Crow grumpily, "neeeeed more sleeeeep!"

He walked around for a few minutes trying to find a quieter corner. "Oh gawd!" he harrumphed, "Shhhh!" The whimpering continued. "You awake One-Eye? – Hedgehog?" he called quietly, trying not to wake any more of the youngsters; still nothing from either of his friends.

As he sat there fed up with the noise, he remembered a song his mother used to sing to him when he was young and scared of the dark, windy nights.

He started to hum the melody, the whimpering ceased and a little voice whispered, "Oh please Mr Bird, sing me a song." Crow started again and, in fact, had a very fine voice. Some of the words were not really for the youngster's little ears, but as he chorused on, so he found himself quite enjoying the nursing role. He sat back reliving his childhood, singing the stories of his past. He didn't notice the crying had been replaced by tiny snores for a long time and, eventually, he crooned himself to sleep.

In the morning, thinking that nobody had heard his moonlit melodies, Crow stomped about, ranting grouchily: "I couldn't sleep for the noise last night, of all the times to break a wing. I can't even escape."

One-Eye leaned towards him on his perch and quietly so no one else could hear, said: "Don't spoil it Crow, you have a beautiful voice and sing well. It's never too late to appreciate children and only natural to be protective of them."

Crow started eating to cover his embarrassment, yet was secretly pleased that his voice wasn't as tuneless as he'd thought it was.

The days that followed passed in a frenzy of feeding, sleeping and lullabies in no particular order. As time went on the youngsters began to feel more secure, but, still, would ask the *same* three questions again and again, which were usually answered by One-Eye with great patience and understanding.

Chapter 8

Go Crow, Go

As the number of orphans and patients in the shed grew, life remained hectic for One-Eye, who was overseeing general activities and doing his best to soothe the troubled mind of each and every new arrival. Nightly sing-songs became a regular feature, with the youngsters always asking to hear more from the three old friends who took it in turns to share their lullabies.

One morning, after a few rounds of feeding had already taken place, Two Legs opened Crow's cage. Although Crow was now more trusting of Two Legs, he resented the intrusion. A hand closed over his body and, lifting him up, started to peel away the sticky band from around his wing.

Momentarily forgetting himself, Crow squawked out "Ouch, that 'urts!" as the tape was peeled away taking a good few of his sleek black flight feathers with it. "Oh my gawd, this wing feels stiff," he thought, "useless!" as he attempted to stretch it out. He was then put into a large cage opposite One-Eye. The Two Legs left and he stomped around his new pen muttering grumpily under his breath at being pulled about so much.

Crow looked down at his wing, "Odd," he thought, "It's no longer hanging at a funny angle, but it still won't move."

"One-Eye," he called "See, it didn't work! I can't move it even though it's not stuck up anymore".

One-Eye remembered only too well the problems he'd had when he first began to heal and said to Crow, "Look at your wing and concentrate very hard on just moving one muscle at a time. Really concentrate."

"Great," thought Crow, "How will 'thinking' help to move it? It either moves or it doesn't and this wing doesn't. All I can do now is flap around in circles," which he promptly did, not concentrating at all, and bumping straight into his water bowl, which provided him with an immediate, and most unwelcome, cold shower. Instinctively, Crow flapped his wings to dispel the water and, sure enough, he noticed that even his injured wing appeared to move a little. He tried again, this time focusing all his attention on the injured wing and yes, it did move.

Again and again he tried, thinking very hard, which made for a very comical sight, as the more he concentrated, the more the feathers on the top of his head stood up, until he looked like he was wearing a top hat, Hedgehog informed One-Eye with a giggle.

Within the day Crow had found that his wing did indeed flap and, although it was now beginning to ache and feel stiff, each time he tried, he was able to move it a little more.

One-Eye, who'd been listening to Crow's efforts all day – repeated flaps, interspersed by moments of concentrated silence – felt very proud of his friend, "Have faith Crow, within a few days you'll be back to normal."

"Then what?" asked Crow.

"I don't know," said One-Eye, honestly "but I feel that it'll be time for you to leave us, and if you do; I have two favours to ask."

"What are they?" asked Crow reluctantly, imagining they were going to be very difficult tasks.

"When you go, firstly; come back from time to time and tell us what's going on out there, and, secondly; if you see any injured creatures, tell them about this place and let them know not to be afraid."

"Well," thought Crow, "That's easy enough."

"Alright," he said.

And, just as One-Eye had suspected, several days later when Crow's wing seemed almost fully recovered, his cage door was left wide open one morning. He peered out, still thinking about cats. "Don't want to go really," he said, scuffing his claws against the floor of his cage.

"Don't be silly" said One-Eye, "You can be of great help to us. Let us know what's going on and keep us up to date with all the latest news."

"Humph," grumbled Crow, who had eaten so well during his stay that he was secretly a little concerned about his return to the skies, even with two fully working wings. He peered around his open cage door again, out into the garden.

"Bye, bye" said Hedgehog, "Good luck."

Even the youngsters, who had been quieter than usual, sensing that something special was going on, piped up,

"Come back and tell us stories, please Mr. Crow, please!"

"Alright," said Crow, who was now preparing to launch himself into the air. "Well, 'ere goes nothin'. Bye mates!" And with one jump, he flew out of the shed into the sunlight.

"Well," said Hedgehog, "That's the last we'll see of him."

"No," said One-Eye, "He'll be back, just wait and see."

"He was nice to me, I'll miss him." added one of the young squirrels, stifling a sniffle.

Moments later, there was a sudden whooshing sound and an almighty '*thud!*' as Crow landed on the outside mesh of One-Eye's cage.

"Don't do that!" cried One-Eye, "You scared me half to death! Next time call when you're coming, please."

"Humph," uttered Crow again "That's a nice greeting!" Giving One-Eye a moment to recover from his shock, while at the same time ensuring that he had the undivided attention of all his friends in the shed, Crow drew himself up to his full height in readiness to deliver his report of the world outside.

"Well, I 'ave to say; this place is bloomin' marvellous!" he informed his audience. "Lots of 'edges, trees, food, water and all sorts... I might just 'ang around 'ere for a while 'til I gets me wing strong enough for some bigger journeys. I'll keep ya posted," and then, once more, out he swooped, narrowly missing a Two Legs who was walking up the garden. "Squawk!" he called out to the Two Legs, "Thank you! You ain't so bad really; look at me wing, it works!"

The Two Legs stopped and held out some food. As Crow flew past, the Two Legs threw the food into the air and Crow, with skilful accuracy, snatched it up in his beak, mid-flight. "Ha!" thought Crow, "Still got all me ol' tricks!" Flying happily out across the hedges, Crow looked down to see what was going on below. "Oh, it's good to be better an' flying *freeee*," he sang as he soared through the air.

Chapter 9

The Rescue

One afternoon, as One-Eye sat having a quick nap between songs, talks and words of reassurances to his charges, he slowly became aware of the sun's heat on his back, its joyous warmth beaming down fondly on his primary feathers. "Oooh, summer comes at last," he thought, smiling to himself.

Life over the past few weeks had been more hectic than he had ever thought possible. With several babies and injured patients arriving at the shed each day, he and Hedgehog had not had a moment's peace.

Crow had been as good as his word and had never strayed too far, often stopping by the shed to pass on the latest

woodland gossip and amuse the youngsters with his somewhat risqué stories, which One-Eye chose to ignore.

Now, hearing Two Legs approaching, Hedgehog looked up, waving her tiny black snout in the air. "Oh heavens," she said, "babies coming! I recognise that piping sound." Sure enough, as the usual box was carefully opened, five very young hedgehogs were revealed, their spines still soft and their eyes tightly shut.

Hedgehog was in her element over the next few hours and the young hogs were notably calmed by her voice, which they recognised to be much like their own mother's. One-Eye listened intently, absorbing his friend's tone and method of communication. He knew that one day Hedgehog would be gone and he would have to cope with such cases alone.

With the latest young arrivals in a warm container and well fed, all was quiet once more and One-Eye waited for the

Two Legs to leave them alone again. Instead, however, to his surprise, he heard his cage door being opened. One-Eye then felt the gentle hands of the Two Legs encircle his body, lifting him slowly out of his enclosure and examining him. Some special bands were being fitted to his legs and, sitting on the Two Legs' hand, to his nervous delight, he was taken out into the warm sunshine.

Although he enjoyed the different noises and events going on all around him, he couldn't understand why he was being taken on this little trip. What if it was the Two Legs' intention to relocate him? One-Eye began to feel very anxious indeed. With him gone, who would look after his friends in the shed, not to mention any new arrivals? Instinctively, One-Eye launched himself into the air and flew blindly in the direction from which he thought he had come. Just then; "I'm flying!" he realised, and, without thinking, he glided in large circles, entranced by the sheer enjoyment of being truly free again. Suddenly, though, he could no longer feel the sun's heat rippling through his feathers and, wavering dangerously, he worried that there must be some object in his path.

"What now?" he thought. Just as the panic threatened to overwhelm him, One-Eye felt a gentle pressure pulling at his legs, which slowed his flight. He was then guided downwards by a mild pressure from the bands. With legs outstretched, sensing the ever-nearing ground, One-Eye awaited a painful crash landing. But, instead, to his relieved astonishment, the bands' pressure seemed to release, bit by bit, just enough that his toes were able to reach downwards and find the floor beneath him.

After a brief moment's pause to confirm he wasn't dreaming, One-Eye launched himself upwards, back into the air, "This is a real miracle," he thought, flying free once again. The same practice was repeated several times over and each time he felt the pressure on his legs, he knew to prepare for a soft landing. Having been in the shed for so long, all this sudden exercise was making One-Eye tired, so, as he was taken back to his home, after what must've been at least a dozen flights, he was exhausted. Exhausted, but happy.

It was shortly after One-Eye's return that Crow made his usual noisy entrance into the shed. He swooped down and, to warn One-Eye of his arrival, squawked, "'Ere I come!" before crashing as loudly as ever into the side of One-Eye's house.

"I saw yer! I saw yer!" he called eagerly, hopping excitedly from foot to foot. "You was on a long string with Two Legs standin' in the middle. Each time yer got near somethin' the Two Legs guided yer down safe. Clever, eh?"

"Yes," said One-Eye, contentedly.

"Anyway," said Crow, "I didn't come 'ere for chitchat, we've got a problem and I don't know what to do." His tiredness all but forgotten, One-Eye was all ears.

"I was flyin' around just now, when I came across a Badger lyin' in a wet place down beside the road. She was groanin' quietly, so I flew down an' asked if I could 'elp. She said that she'd been 'it by a Lightnin' Thunder last night and can't move 'er back legs at all. An' she's frettin', see, cos 'er baby's a little way away in a nearby field." Crow paused to get his breath back. "So, I flew to where she said 'er baby was, an' showed the littl'un back to 'er mother. She was very scared, the littl'un, but she followed me. She was able to get a bit a milk from 'er mum, but she's still 'ungry, so now I got real bother. The baby's cryin' an' the mother's in a bad way. What shall I do?"

One-Eye sat perfectly still for a while, turning the problem over in his mind. Silently, he called to the Great Tree Owl for help and slowly came the Great One's reply; "Use the Two Legs' friends."

One-Eye continued to sit quietly, trying to understand the meaning of the message. Gradually, he began to realise what the plan of action must be.

"Crow," he said "I've got a solution, but I don't know if you're brave enough."

"Me?" said Crow, incredulously "'Course I am!" Crow, who would never admit to being scared, secretly wondered just how brave he was going to have to be.

"Go to the Two Legs' friends," said One-Eye "and ask them if they'll help us."

"You don't mean the dogs?" said Crow, going visibly pale. "I ain't speakin' to no dogs! You know we always steer well clear of them."

"Well," said One-Eye, "When you think about it, have they ever done us any harm? Even as I landed on the ground, when I was out flying, though I could sense them right there in front of me, I felt no danger at all. So, this is what you must do ...

Chapter 10

A Difficult Plan

Crow flew out across the garden and sat in a nearby tree, waiting for the dogs to come past. He didn't like this plan at all. Not one bit. At length, the two dogs came wandering by...

"Psst," said Crow. The dogs looked around and, not seeing anything, strolled on. "'Ere you," Crow called again, "It's me, Crow, up in the tree."

"Oh yes, we see you now, what do you require?"

Most polite, thought Crow, and posh too. "Well," said Crow, "We got a bit of a problem and think you can 'elp us... what d'ya say?" he paused as the dogs looked at each other, obviously thinking that Crow was quite mad.

Crow plucked up the courage, puffed himself out and continued with his tale. "Just across the field is an injured badger, real poorly she is, an' I need to get the Two Legs to go over an' rescue 'er."

"Oh," said the dogs, trotting over to the tree and jumping their front paws up onto its trunk to get a little closer to Crow, who hopped up a couple of branches higher, just to be on the safe side.

"What can we do?" asked the dogs.

"Well, I want you to attract the Two Legs' attention an' then jump over the fence. Go round the bottom of the field to where the badger is lyin' an' make the Two Legs bring 'er back 'ere."

"Not so easy," said one of the dogs, "We never go out alone and certainly would not jump over the fence, that would get us into terrible trouble."

"Oh dear," said Crow, dejected.

"However," the dog continued, "We'll give the matter some thought and try to come up with a plan, after all, we don't do much to help you lot in the shed."

"Great," said Crow, "Gimme a bark when you're ready an' I'll tell you where ta go."

A short while later, the dogs reappeared and called to Crow.

"Alright" they said, "We've worked out a way of getting Two Legs to come across the field with us. You'll have to fly in front and lead the way until we pick up the scent. Follow us down the garden and wait for Two Legs to join us and then, when we get into the field, fly on ahead."

So, their strategy decided, the two dogs set off down the garden towards the gate, with Crow flying just above them, feeling very brave indeed.

Suddenly, the dogs started barking, causing Crow to almost jump out of his feathers. But the noise enticed Two Legs out of the house to make loud sounds at the dogs, who proceeded back and forth, barking and whining, getting nearer and nearer to the gate of the field as they did so. The dogs jumped up at the gate and then back to the Two Legs, back and forth they leapt, barking all the while.

Eventually, the Two Legs opened the gate, as if suddenly understanding, and followed the dogs out into the field. Crow flew forward then, swooping down across the field. The dogs followed Crow's directions and soon picked up the scent of the Badger. Instinct took over as they darted through the long grass and came to a standstill beside the hedge, barking loudly and wagging their tails. Looking up at them through the undergrowth was the injured badger and her baby, who had now scurried under her mother's legs in fright.

The Two Legs came closer to see what the reason was for all the dogs' noise.

"Great work!" said Crow. But his delight was short-lived, as, immediately, the Two Legs turned around and ran straight back across the field. In his frustration, Crow, quite forgetting himself, hopped down and sat on one of the dogs' heads.

"Well that's not so great," he said, "Now what?"

"Don't worry," said the dog, "and please don't sit on my head. They've seen the problem and will be back any moment."

Sure enough, shortly after that, the Two Legs returned with another Two Legs, huffing and puffing, and carrying two large box-like objects, long poles and various other things. Whilst the first Two Legs stepped down through the hedge and put a band attached to a long pole around the mother badger's neck, terrifying her, the other plucked the baby up by the scruff and carried her away, back to the garden.

The mother badger, still fighting hard, was prevented from moving very much by the pole instrument, which was positioned firmly around her neck. The Two Legs then produced something sharp from his pocket that he pushed into the mother badger, who instantly became silent and still. She too was then lifted into a box and carried back through the gate, where she was put directly into the Lightning Thunder, which drove off at great speed.

Meanwhile, the dogs and Crow returned to the shed, where the baby badger was being placed in a large cage full of straw, blankets and a large red, hot light.

All the inhabitants of the shed watched quietly as the new arrival was settled in her pen, and took great pity on the poor whimpering baby.

"My mother's dead and gone," she cried pitifully, and crept into a distant corner of the strange new home she found herself in, to hide herself amongst the straw.

As soon as the Two Legs was gone, One-Eye called across to the baby, "Don't be afraid little one; your mother will be alright. The Two Legs are good and will look after you, but

first you must be strong. When they come back they will try to feed you. Conquer your fear and take the food. You must then be patient and brave, until your mother comes back."

One-Eye started to sing softly to the youngster, who slowly edged forward under the warm light and curled up to sleep, not knowing what the future would bring.

Chapter 11

Reunited

After only a short while, the Two Legs returned and started their usual round of feeding. The young orphaned birds gaped keenly at the sight of the now familiar food-bearing tweezers and the tiny piping hedgehogs waved their little noses excitedly in the milk-scented air. The squirrels were also still being fed by the Two Legs, even though they were really just being lazy and could quite easily have fed by themselves from the bowl of food that was always left in front of them.

One-Eye sat and listened to the happy mealtime sounds of his 'family' around him. He could see them all now quite clearly in his mind's eye (and with a little descriptive help from his friends Hedgehog and the ever-appearing Crow).

One-Eye could place each tiny noise and its whereabouts with ease and, such was his accuracy; many of those in the shed did not even realise that he was blind.

All the while his own strength came from the voice within him.

As everyone was finishing up the last of their lunch, One-Eye started to become concerned that no attention had been paid to the little badger cub, who had remained asleep despite all the noise and clamour of feeding time in the shed. Just then, however, the Two Legs came back in, knelt down and opened the baby badger's cage door. Instead of reaching for the young cub, the Two Legs moved the hot light so that it shone out to where he now sat, very quietly in the middle of the shed floor.

The young badger instinctively stirred when she no longer felt the heat of the light on her body and, without realising it, muzzled forward to seek out its warmth again. Hedgehog watched too, fascinated that the Two Legs had made no movement whatsoever from where he sat. The cub soon found the heat and, had she been more awake, would have realised that its source was in fact the Two Legs' lap. Quietly, then, she began to cry, as if she were unsure of the new smell that suddenly surrounded her. One-Eye called over encouragingly in his soft, melodic voice, "Trust your new friends, don't be scared."

Hedgehog continued to observe as the Two Legs poured some milk into his hand and held it very still just in front of the young badger's nose. Her little black nostrils twitched, sniffed and twitched again. This was a smell she recognised but there was also something else, a scent that sparked an innate fear within her. Though she paused briefly, hunger fast overcame her worries and she lent forwards to sample the delicacy. The Two Legs stayed perfectly still, waiting quietly as if knowing that it would take time for the orphaned cub to brave her anxiety. Little by little, very slowly, the cub relaxed forward until her tiny snout was submerged in the warm milk. Out came her pink tongue, lapping gently at first and then with greater enthusiasm as she realised how very hungry she was.

As she drank, so the Two Legs carefully flowed milk into his cupped palm, until the cub was had had her fill. Her belly delightfully satisfied, showing no fear now, she stretched her legs and nuzzled into the Two Legs' clothes, seeking a warm dark place in which to rest.

The whole scene had been quite hypnotic; all the inmates sensing, and empathising with, the young badger's struggle between her inbuilt wariness of Two Legs and her need for food.

A magic moment, thought One-Eye, who had listened to the cub's contented 'slurping' sounds with pride for the little one's courage. The youngster was then carefully lifted up and put back in her cage, the heat replaced and a blanket wrapped around her for extra warmth.

Regular rounds of feeding continued throughout the day, until dusk fell and all the inhabitants of the shed began to settle down for the night. Suddenly, the young badger jumped up, immediately alert, crying out and calling for her mother.

"Hush little one," called One-Eye, soothingly.

"No! You don't understand" she squealed, "She's coming! She's coming!"

It was only then that One-Eye heard the Two Legs approaching and detected the adult badger's scent getting closer. He wondered whether his incredible hearing was failing him or whether the youngster was using her special sense to alert her to her mother's presence.

The shed door opened and another Two Legs appeared, cradling the adult badger in his arms. Quickly, he knelt down and put the badger in with her cub, who made a cautious approach, worried by her mother's stillness. Despite a tentative, gentle nudge, her mother didn't even stir, causing the youngster to whimper again, yet, as she knew there was no smell of death, she snuggled up close and lay waiting.

Slowly the adult badger opened her eyes, smiled and whispered to her baby, "Don't fear little one, all is well. I've had a very strange dream which I will tell you about later. I must sleep now, but are you hungry?"

"No mother, I'm well fed," said the cub.

"Good," sighed her mother, immediately drifting back into her heavy sleep. The young badger crept even closer then and curled up in between her mother's fore legs, sighing with contentment and knowing that she was back where she belonged.

Chapter 12

The Road to Recovery and the Sudden Farewell

Whilst the mother badger slept, the Two Legs fed the young cub several times. Following each feeding she would scurry back to the safety of her mother's soft belly fur. The bond that tied them was only ever temporarily broken and the Two Legs did their utmost not to damage it in any way. The cub always thoroughly washed herself after each meal and, as her mother lay in slumber, she considered it her duty to bathe her too. It was during one of these sessions that the mother badger, feeling her youngster's tongue carefully cleansing her snout, finally

awoke. She was delighted to see her baby in such good health, though, considering her own misfortune, she feared for her youngster's future. Certainly, she felt much better than she had when Crow had found her in the field, but she knew only too well how serious her injuries were. The healing process would take many weeks and this was time which she did not have.

Being an adult badger, she had an innate fear of Two Legs, so, although her youngster appeared unharmed, she knew she would not be able to entrust them with her and her baby's care. But she also knew that she was not well enough to find food to feed either of them herself. She began to worry about how to explain all these things to her child. Slowly, she crawled forward across her cage; she had no feeling in, and, therefore, no use of, her hind legs, so even these small movements caused her great hardship.

The young cub, though not understanding her mother's difficulties, couldn't fail to notice her pained expression. "We must talk," said the mother to her baby, "I'm afraid I have little chance of survival and so you, who are reliant on me, are going to have to be very brave."

One-Eye, who had been listening, realised at once what she was saying and called across to interrupt her conversation. The mother badger snapped back at One-Eye and growled. What she had to say was difficult enough without being disturbed. Again One-Eye called out in his hypnotic way, begging her to wait and to listen for just a few minutes to what he had to say before she continued. Very angrily she said, "Oh, very well, if you must keep interrupting, I suppose a few minutes will not matter."

One-Eye spoke of his accident, his time at the shed and of the many patients who came and went. He spoke also of the way that the badger and her youngster came to be there. The badger, at first, was bewildered and confused, but she listened intently to the story. In all her life she had only known of cruelty and persecution by the Two Legs and this new tale was astounding her. Once One-Eye had finished, she appeared visibly calmer and there were tears of hope welling in her eyes. She looked at her baby who did indeed seem to be well fed, despite her inability to provide for her in recent days.

As if on cue, the Two Legs appeared and, while still trying to come to terms with these new ideas, the badger buried herself a bit deeper in her straw bedding. The fear would take a long time to subside.

The badgers' cage was opened and the youngster left to come out for food in her own time. She looked round at her mother for permission to go and with a reluctant trust, her mother nodded her approval. The next thing she heard was her youngster slurping loudly on her meal. While the cage door was open, a larger bowl of food was placed in front of her. A magnificent scent invaded her nostrils, but still her innate fear prevented her from coming forward. It was not until the Two Legs had left and her youngster was safely back beside her, that she allowed herself to take those first, hesitant, but wonderfully welcome, mouthfuls of food. She hadn't eaten for a long time, so it wasn't very long before she had gobbled up what would usually amount to four or five meals. As she lay back, her appetite sated, for the first time she felt that the faith instilled into her by One-Eye was genuine and that everything might indeed work out for the best. She licked her child, who fell into a contented sleep under the reassuring caress of her mother's soft tongue.

Over time, the mother badger swapped many stories with One-Eye and Hedgehog. A close friendship began to develop between the three animals and, as each came to share more wise tales of their past lives of freedom, so they all began to understand that from this place of captivity, there was also hope.

Crow, as always, paid them regular fleeting visits during the days, keeping them up-to-date with life on the outside, until one morning a great surprise came to them all. Quite out of the blue, Hedgehog was taken out of her cage and out of the shed. There followed great unrest in the shed, as everyone wondered whether they'd ever see her again.

The Two Legs had been carrying out their usual morning rounds. Hedgehog was now very used to being picked up and having her tummy examined, but, if the truth be

known, she had really given very little thought to ever leaving; she quite enjoyed life in the shed with her new friends and the luxury of having her meals delivered directly to her without the need to hunt or forage. So, when she was placed into an unfamiliar, dark box, only the memory of One-Eye's continued words of reassurance prevented her from going into a complete panic. She had little time for farewells and only managed a quick, "Thank you" to One-Eye, and "Good Luck!" to all of her friends, before the lid was closed and she was taken away from the smells and sounds she had grown to think of as home.

Chapter 13

Back to the Wild

Having little idea of how much time had elapsed, Hedgehog looked up as the lid of her new box was removed and the scent of early evening flooded in, filling the space around her. A Two Legs' hand reached down then, lifting her out of the box and placing her gently on the ground beside a bowl of food, which was stationed just outside a tunnel entrance.

Two Legs stepped back and waited. She sniffed around and ambled through the long meadow grass, the like of which she had been used to all her life. Although pleased to be free, Hedgehog was saddened that she had not been able to say a proper goodbye to her friends and, if she were honest, also more than a little anxious about her new, unfamiliar surroundings.

The Two Legs lent down and, without picking her up, steered Hedgehog lightly in the direction of the tunnel she had just seen. It was not until she was quite close to the entrance that she smelt it had been built by them, and, given that she now had considerably less fear of the Two Legs, she trundled happily into the darkness, as was obviously expected of her. Though not a long tunnel, it was quite tight, which made it small enough to prevent any of her natural enemies from following her inside. At the end of the tunnel was a chamber just the right size for a hedgehog's home and already there was a covering of dry leaves which would make the perfect bed!

When she re-emerged into the twilight, Hedgehog found that she was completely alone, yet the bowl of food was still in place, she noted. Another wander around assured her that there were no bars, no doors such as those which had upset her so much when she first arrived in the shed.

Hedgehog's unaccustomed excursion had made her hungry, so she set about sampling the content of her food bowl. But, just as she was about to take her first bite, a sudden 'Whoosh!' from above gave her such a start that she instinctively went to curl into a tight ball, accidentally catching her nose on the bowl's rim as she did so, and catapulting a large amount of food clean over her own head. A black shape swooped down over her from a great height.

"Cor blimey!" said Crow, who was now standing at her side, "Food not up to scratch out 'ere?"

Hedgehog laughed, a little embarrassed. "What're you doing out an' about anyway? Everyone's been proper worried about you. They're upset too, 'cause they didn't even 'ave the chance to say goodbye."

Hedgehog, who had not quite recovered from her own shock, squeaked, "But how did you find me so quickly, Crow? You must have flown for miles! I'm so glad to see you."

Crow started to giggle. Then he laughed… and coughed… and laughed a bit more, until he toppled over completely. In fact, it was only because he fell against Hedgehog's prickly spines that his guffawing was halted long enough for him to say, "Ouch, that 'urt!"

"Well?" said Hedgehog, who was becoming increasingly frustrated at not understanding what was so funny, "Isn't it really far away?"

Thankfully, Crow had started to calm down a bit, "Come over 'ere. Follow me," he said, and he walked a short distance, through a gap in the hedge and pointed with his wing. "Look," he said, "See that?"

Hedgehog did not have very good long-distance sight, but could make out a blur not so very far away.

"Yeeess" said Hedgehog, "I think so."

Crow started to laugh again.

"Oh, do be quiet," said Hedgehog.

Crow shook himself and said, "Look, that's where you've been with the others all this time, just over there!"

Hedgehog was quite choked with happiness. "Oh dear," she said, "and there I was thinking I'd travelled over hills and dales!"

"Well then," said Crow, fondly, "I can now report that all's well, can't I?"

"Oh do!" said Hedgehog, "and tell them I'll come and visit them tonight when I've sorted out my new home."

"Okey dokey," said Crow, "and by the way, just so you know, over there's a big field surrounded by nice thick 'edges," and, pointing with his wing again, "an' over that way there's a big pond with a small wood behind."

"Hmm, should be excellent for finding food," said Hedgehog, and even more perfect for bringing up a family sometime in the future too, she thought.

With that, Crow launched himself into the air with effortless ease and called out, "See ya tonight, Hog. Enjoy ya new 'ouse!" as he disappeared into the distance.

Hedgehog now felt truly happy; she was back out in the wild again, yet near enough to her old friends to visit whenever she felt like it. What could be better, she thought, as she scurried off into the tunnel of her new home with a little smile on her face.

Crow, meanwhile, had flown back to One-Eye and friends to impart the good news and had them all – including Badger – laughing uncontrollably when he'd told them of Hedgehog's food-flinging shock at his sudden appearance next to her in the field. (He left out the part about falling against her prickles because he thought it made him seem silly.)

Hearing all the noise from the shed, the dogs walked over and stuck their noses round the door, "Anything wrong?" they asked.

"No," said Crow, who then recounted the story all over again.

The dogs were now quite frequent visitors to the shed, always asking if there was anything they could do to help. They had enjoyed their part in the rescue of Badger and often trotted in to see her young cub, of whom they were particularly fond.

"Alright," they said, adding to Crow as they turned to leave; "Remember, anything you ever need, you know where to find us."

Good friends, thought One-Eye, when they had gone. They could be very useful to us one day. Already a plan was forming in his mind, but he could not yet quite put it all together. He hoped that one of his dreams would eventually give him the guidance he needed.

Chapter 14

Rehabilitation

That evening was the first time that Hedgehog had been alone for a long while. She had spent the few remaining daylight hours rearranging her new home and collecting some extra soft bedding for her sleeping quarters. She had also done a little investigating; searching out the nearest hedgerows that would make suitable hiding places, should she ever find herself in danger when away from the safety of her home. Her surrounding area was proving perfect for her needs and she found that she was adapting very quickly to her resumed natural life.

During her time outside, Hedgehog had, on several occasions, been sure to stand quite still, listening carefully to see if she was in any danger from Lightning Thunders, but could only hear their low rumbles in the far, far distance. She certainly had not yet come across any of the barren, dangerous places that she had learnt about from the other wild creatures, where the Lightning Thunders reigned. How wise some of the worldly tips she had been given during her time of capture were and how grateful she was now to have been told of them.

Her time with the Two Legs would stand her in good stead for the future. She did, though, miss the regular meals that she hadn't even had to hunt for and only realised, as she was huffing and puffing over a nearby hillock, that it was probably just as well she was going to have to start foraging for food again, because she certainly had put on a little too much weight of late!

As dusk's hue deepened – a time hedgehogs usually set aside for hunting – she was feeling rather tired from all her activity and, instead of searching for food, she decided to crawl into her bed for a quick nap. No sooner had she fallen asleep, when there came a loud tapping noise on her roof, followed by an irritated carking sound, "Where are you?" called Crow, who had now flown down and stuck his head into the tunnel entrance.

"Come in," she called, having now recognised her visitor to be Crow.

"Not likely!" he called back, "I ain't comin' in there; you can't see nothin'!"

"Ha ha, scardey Crow!" Hedgehog taunted,

"No, I'm not!" he retaliated, "I just don't like the dark,

that's all. Besides, you said you were comin' down to see us all tonight."

"Yes, I am going to," said Hedgehog, "but later."

Crow was already looking around nervously; it was not far from darkness and definitely not a time when crows should be flying around.

"I'm off now," he called, "See ya later."

"'Bye," said Hedgehog, who had reached the opening of the tunnel entrance just in time to see Crow soar up into the air and disappear over the top of the hedge. It was then that she heard the familiar approach of a Two Legs nearby. Instincts, not quite forgotten, seemed to have returned quickly, because before she even realised it she had rolled up into a tight ball, as was her natural reflex at a stranger's approach. From within the safety of her prickly defences, however, she heard the welcome sound of food being scooped into the bowl that had been left out for her, next to her new home. Hedgehog uncurled just enough to stick out her snout and see what was going on. Hmm, not as much nosh as usual, but she would be glad of the small meal provided, should her first night's hunting not be successful. Hedgehog decided to eat just a little of the food and leave the rest for her return journey. So, after a tasty two mouthfuls she set off to visit her friends.

One-Eye, in the meantime, had been preoccupied with forming his plan, in addition to putting the minds of two new inmates to rest and explaining to them that all would be well. He had also had time for a longer talk with Badger and it was obvious that, although she had been feeling much better and less tired, she was very concerned that she still had no feeling in the back half of her body.

"Time," One-Eye had reassured her, "Rest and time. I had the same trouble for many moons before I could even swallow properly, let alone move about. Trust the Two Legs; they know what they're doing."

All the usual routines continued; the regular feeding and the scrupulous cleaning, day in and day out. And then the morning arrived when the Two Legs carried out their first close inspection of the adult badger, which proved to be a very hazardous experience.

Despite her door being slowly and quietly opened and knowing that she must accept their intrusion as it was for her own good, her natural instincts still proved too strong. As the Two Legs leant forward to examine her, she turned her head and snapped wildly at their hands. They didn't panic, which surprised her, but instead calmly stepped back and collected a long pole machine, which they smoothly placed around her neck. This prevented her from moving her head while they came in closer once again, to look at her back legs. It was a strange sensation for Badger, who, out of the corner of her eye, could see them manipulating and massaging her limbs, but yet could feel nothing. Her baby looked on nervously and, sensing her mother's fear, she backed off into the far corner of their cage.

"Don't fear little one," said Badger, repeating One-Eye's earlier words. "They are only trying to help," and though she continued to growl quietly, she made no effort to hurt the Two Legs, who spent a long time rubbing her numb legs and moving them back and forth.

Once the Two Legs had left for the evening, the animals and birds, as pre-warned by Crow, sat and waited for Hedgehog, who arrived very out of breath and regretting her last quick meal. As she scuttled in through the doorway, it was One-Eye who bid her the first greeting, although the others quickly joined in with much enthusiasm. The baby hedgehogs all clambered forward towards her, as if she had been away for years and immediately started bombarding her with questions. She told them of her new home and the surrounding land and also that the Two Legs, even now, had not forgotten her because they still provided her with a little food.

The evening was spent, as usual, with the swapping of stories and the singing of a great many woodland songs. It wasn't until long after the middle night that hedgehog bade them all a fond farewell. Crow, however, took one look outside into the darkness and declared that he had decided to stay with his friends for the night, to keep them company. He then flew up and perched on a ledge next to One-Eye, who shuffled over to make room for his friend.

As Hedgehog made her way home, enjoying the cool night air and the dew on the grass, she was feeling most content.

Chapter 15

The End and the Beginning

The occupants of the hospital grew quiet. Crow, with his head under his wing, became still. The baby hedgehogs, after their exciting evening, all scuttled back to their warm bedding and snuggled up together, while the young badger curled up between her mother's legs. Soon, all were fast asleep. All, that is, apart from One-Eye, whose mind was troubled.

He silently paced up and down on his perch thinking about his plan, until, eventually, sleep overcame him too and he closed his eyes and fell into a deep slumber.

"One-Eye, One-Eye," the voice came quietly but insistently, "See how well you have done? You have advised, calmed and helped so many of our friends. Those who have left us remember you with great affection and you have won the confidence of all who have met you. Now, let us think more deeply about your plan and, together, decide how best to proceed."

"Proceed with what?" dreamt One-Eye.

"Oh brave one, think what effect you could have if you were able to help save more and more injured and orphaned creatures, give them a chance that they would not otherwise have, let them know that there are Two Legs here that will help. The word must be spread and this is how we will go about it..."

Long into the night, although One-Eye was asleep, his feathers twitched and his beak moved, as if he were speaking urgently! By morning, when he came to stretch his wings in the early light, he had a calm and happy expression on his face. Once everyone was awake, he announced that it was an important day and that there was much to organise.

So, when the first session of feeding was over and the Two Legs had left, he called Crow to fetch the dogs and Hedgehog and any friends they, together, could find. He had particular instructions to give everyone in preparation for the coming darkness, when there was to be a very special meeting.

There was frenzied activity throughout the day. Not only did One-Eye invite all their friends to the meeting, but also any animal or bird who happened to pass by. In addition to this, all friends were asked to call to as many of their own kind as possible to advise them of the planned gathering.

This caused much ado during the course of the day, because as soon as the Two Legs had left them, each inmate would take their turn to call out. One-Eye was worried when it came Badger's turn to call, but she managed to drag herself to a sitting position and, having warned everyone to block their ears, she started to make the loudest noises you could possibly imagine! A mixture of barking, growling and whining. In fact, Badger managed to cause such a racket that not long after she had started, the Two Legs came running up to the shed, obviously worried that there was something terribly wrong. Badger stopped calling and adopted an, "I'm quite alright, thank you" face, and then as soon as they left, she started again. Even the dogs were getting into trouble that day, as they spent most of their time standing by the hedge, barking the message to all who would listen, ignoring the Two Legs' constant attempts to quieten them down.

It was only Crow who caused no problems. He had been sent off very early by One-Eye to fly around the area, as far as he could go, and ask creatures who had already been released to come back to listen to One-Eye's message.

By the time Crow returned, he had not even the breath to announce his arrival in the usual way, instead, simply flopping down on the floor and falling immediately to sleep. It was not until the Two Legs came in to feed everyone that he finally awoke and quietly crept off into a corner, to continue his well-earned rest. He was quite touched when, after the Two Legs had left for the evening, he found that they'd placed a bowl of food and water at his side.

The time seemed to pass very slowly, with everyone waiting expectantly to see who would turn up at the shed. It was only One-Eye who seemed unconcerned as he crept to the side of his perch for a little nap. As darkness fell, so the creatures started arriving. First to appear was Hedgehog, who had begun her slow walk down to the shed earlier in the afternoon, rounding up as many of the young fledglings who had been gathered in nearby hedgerows as she could, on her way. It was a very comical sight to see them all file through the door, one by one, under Hedgehog's charge, with several squirrel families bringing up the rear, to make sure that no one got lost along the way.

Crow, now awake, had slipped up beside One-Eye and was (quite uncharacteristically, for him) quietly announcing each arrival into One-Eye's ear. One-Eye appeared to take very little notice, not even opening his eyes but just nodding his head in occasional acknowledgement. By mid-darkness, the area was full of creatures all talking in hushed tones, as they did not wish to wake the wise old owl. (If the Two Legs had walked in, they would have received the most incredible surprise!)

Even the two dogs were in attendance, sitting amiably to either side of the doorway. There were birds perched everywhere, on every available ledge, with some even finding the courage to line up along Badger's back. Badger, thankfully, was being exceedingly tolerant.

One-Eye, very slowly, opened his sightless eyes and shook his feathers. As he moved to the centre of his perch, however,

fear engulfed him. From Crow, he had learnt that he had an audience of over a hundred expectant faces. He sat frozen to the spot, forgetting everything he was going to say.

But then, gradually, a feeling of blessed warmth began to surge through him and he felt the presence of the Great Tree Owl surround him. He raised himself to his full majestic height and began to speak.

"My dear friends," he began, his voice sounding vibrantly strong. "Thank you for being here this mid-darkness. Many of you will know of the work done here and the help given to those of us who have been through a time of suffering, be it through illness, accident or injury. Now it is our turn to assist others who, at any time, may need the same help. We must make them aware of this place, where the Two Legs are kind, and support them in overcoming their natural fears, to trust in our experiences."

One-Eye's resonant voice now held the room, the strength he felt from the Great Tree Owl filling him with courage and sincerity.

"When you leave here, tell every friend you meet that this place is a true sanctuary. A place where they can come for care. A place where Two Legs can be trusted. A place of healing. Tell them that if ever they are in trouble, they should call out for help and, somehow, we will find a way of getting them here. Tell them we are waiting for them, to give them our courage and our strength."

Not a sound. Not a flutter. Not even a squeak could be heard as One-Eye's great prophecy began to sink in. One-Eye was right of course. Had it not been for the caring Two

Legs, hardly any of the creatures assembled in that mid-darkness would have had a chance of the healthy recovery they now knew. News of the good work carried out by this special place did indeed need to be shared with others. The stillness of those gathered was slowly broken by this realisation. Nods of approval, rustles of recognition grew into an excited twittering, squawking, hooting and barking; a frenzied crescendo that became so loud there was a real danger that the Two Legs themselves would be alerted before long.

And so it was that from that very first meeting, Wildlife Aid was born. Henceforth, many more stories of rescue would, ever after, be echoed throughout the Animal Kingdom thanks to the vision of the owl with the Golden Heart.

<u>Survivors' Tales:</u>
<u>Fox's Story</u>

Fox Foxed

Fox stopped and sat panting, his great pink tongue lolling to one side of his mouth. He was very tired. A bad night's hunting overall and in terrible conditions. The rain had been falling constantly since dark and now dawn was fast approaching; his magnificent coat was hidden under a generous coating of mud and sludge. He stood up and vigorously shook his body, dispelling droplets of water in a great arc about himself. Despite his lack of success, Fox always enjoyed his night excursions over the land which he knew so well. His nightly routine kept him well clear of any possible contact with Two Legs and, being a very clever fox, he only crossed barren, sterile places when absolutely necessary, keeping a very wary eye open for the Lightning Thunders that roared down such corridors.

He looked around and decided it was time to return to his den, where he would spend the morning resting and telling his children exaggerated tales of his exploits. He smiled to himself as several stories sprang to mind, and, as he walked back across a ditch, under an old rusting fence and up into the nearby copse, he thought about the days ahead and his plans to find a new home for his family.

At the other side of the copse was an extremely dense blanket of brambles and a very old blackthorn hedge that he usually avoided because, however careful he was, he often received a painfully deep scratch from one of the many hideous barbs. As he skirted this area, a scent crossed his nose – a possible meal – from somewhere just in front, up-wind of him. Fox crouched down, waiting to locate its source and considered a suitable plan of attack. He remained perfectly still, his eyes scanning the area for any movement while his nose eagerly awaited a fresh scent. There, out of the corner of his eye, he saw it. Just the slightest movement. His quarry then froze in time with him once more.

Fox weighed up the situation. The quarry was halfway through the bramble layer, facing in the direction of the dreaded blackthorn; whichever angle Fox entered, the only escape route would be a thorny one indeed. But, Fox considered, the promise of a tasty meal was worth risking a few cuts and scratches for. Fox waited, other than the slight quiver of excitement, he was as still as the night, as

he chose his moment of attack. The quarry moved again, obviously thinking that any danger had passed. Fox took a deep breath and prepared for the chase. Whoosh! He leapt forward, landing only a few feet away from his likely dinner. As he did so, the rabbit darted sideways and easily slipped beneath the bramble layer, towards the blackthorn. Fox followed, hardly noticing as the brambles scraped his face and legs. So close – just one foot – and his jaws would close on supper! The rabbit swerved towards a small gap in the blackthorn hedge and Fox slewed round to follow. Too late, he suddenly sensed the vague presence of Two Legs' scent. He was one tantalising crunch away as he fluidly

lowered his body to follow the rabbit under the hedge. But, before he knew it, he was snapped to an abrupt halt, just as his jaws opened to take his prey. "Damn!" he thought, stuck in a small 'V' of branches. The rabbit was clear.

Fox pulled back to release himself, yet still the branches held fast. Desperately he squirmed, both this way and that, backwards and forwards, but the more he struggled the less he could move his neck. The panic that now coursed through him was absolute. Feeling no pain from the blackthorn, he thrashed wildly in all directions to try to work himself free, serving only to squeeze his trapped neck still tighter. His eyes were beginning to fog and he was breathing in hardly more than a grating rasp. Pain crept over his body and his limbs shook with weakness and fear.

Fox had no alternative but to stop and re-think. Little did he know that this was the best thing he could have done, for when he stopped, breathless and exhausted, so the pressure around his neck released just enough for him to gulp down a few precious lungfuls of beautiful fresh air.

As his terror-filled eyes quickly darted from side to side, only then did he catch a glimpse of shiny wire which seemed to be anchored securely to the base of a large trunk of the hedge. Each time he moved, the wire glinted in the half-light. He should rest a while to regain his strength and then try again. Fox lay down, feeling not only the bruising pain round his neck but the many lacerations to his body, where the blackthorn had bitten viciously into every inch of his skin. He smelt his own blood. Fox whimpered quietly, as a tear ran silently down his nose.

Safety and Recovery

The frantic energy Fox had expended at least let him sleep for a while. Only when he heard the clonk! of a Lightning Thunder door in the distance did he wake up and, instinctively, begin to thrash around once more, to be rid of his deadly trap.

The nearing of a Two Legs and his dog only made Fox even more panic-stricken. As the dog, attracted by the scent and noise, ran to greet him, Fox literally jumped in somersaults to be free. His agony was now so devastating that he could not breathe. His eyes, bulging and red with pain, searched sightlessly for any escape. His strength ebbed from him and he slithered, unconscious, to the ground.

Though Fox had no recollection of anything that had occurred before he collapsed, when he finally did regain consciousness, his panic was not lessened. He smelt Two Legs' scent and was surprised that it was, once again, darkness. But where was he? Wherever it was, it was moving and noisy. Mingled with the Two Legs' scent was also that of two dogs. Fox's neck and body, albeit still agonising, at least appeared no worse. It was more out of fear than pain that he now yelped, as he lay awaiting his fate.

Not long afterwards, the surrounding motion ceased and the noise quietened. Fox waited. The sound of Two Legs came nearer, so he crouched down in his prison. A slit of light appeared and he could see three pairs of eyes looking at him. Fox growled a fierce, menacing growl, which rumbled from deep within his throat. Still the eyes looked but made no approach. He waited, terrified, but ready to fight for his life if necessary. The slither of brightness disappeared but was soon replaced by another one which shone right into his face. Then, a tube with a pointed metallic spike on the end of it appeared; he swung round and bit deeply into the apparent weapon as it came steadily towards him, alas, to no avail. It was not withdrawn, as he had expected, but just left, unmoving.

His attack on it having had no effect, he didn't bother to pursue his assault, but backed away as far as he could into the darkest available corner. As the tube met his rump he felt a sharp pain, which sent him wild again. The light now disappeared and he lay waiting for a chance to escape.

It was strange how all his senses started to dull. He felt sleepy and weak and as the light, yet again, reappeared, he was amazed by how little it seemed to worry him. Out of the light there came a hand, reaching towards him and, although he made a half-hearted attempt at a growl, he was astonished to find that he wasn't overly concerned with that either. It was as if he was asleep but could still see and hear everything going on around him. The hand moved forward lifting him gently into the Two Legs' arms, where he was carried through a door and laid down onto a table.

At least the pain in his body seemed to be much less, he thought dozily. The hands worked over his body and came to rest on his neck. With one sudden snipping noise, at last he felt the restriction that had been strangling him, free. Some vile-smelling liquid was poured over his wounds and, although it stung slightly, he sensed it was for his own good. More time was spent examining his body; various places were rubbed with the vile-smelling liquid and finally, after one more wasp-like stinging pain in his back leg, he slept.

Waking up again proved a very slow process for Fox, as he struggled to fight off his heavy sleep. The smells that surrounded him now were different, more natural to him. He was lying on something soft and warm and could smell other creatures around him, hear low murmuring noises – noises he recognised. He shook his head, in an attempt to clear his mind, regretting such a move instantly for the physical pain it caused him.

"Hello… Wake up, sleepyhead…" called One-Eye, in a low voice. "No need to speak, just stay calm now and listen to what I say."

Fox could not believe what was happening, convinced that he must be dreaming. One-Eye continued, "You are safe here. All is not as it may seem. You are among friends and will be cared for until you are well enough to return to your home. I am told that your neck looks damaged and that you have a deep cut all the way round it, but do not fear, all will be well. Two Legs may approach you. Try not to panic; they will do you no harm. Accept what is given and concentrate on getting your body well again."

Fox let his eyelids close again and slept, for he was still very drowsy. He awoke only at the sound of a Two Legs approaching and quickly crept to the back of his enclosure. Instinctively, a low rumbling sound emerged from the well of his throat. It wasn't until he smelt food that he realised how hungry he was. The Two Legs placed the food to the far side of his cage. He looked longingly at it but dared not to move. The Two Legs went away and Fox lay waiting. One-Eye spoke again, "You see, no harm has come to you and there is fresh food for you to eat."

Fox inched forward, but realised as he moved his head that he would be unable to eat; the pain all around his neck and inside his throat was far too great to allow him to swallow. He edged towards the bowl and was amazed to see that it contained not hard lumps of food, but more like a thick watery substance. Cautiously, he lapped at the mixture with his swollen tongue. It tasted like the meat he so loved, but was soft and runny enough that it passed easily down his sore throat. Carefully and slowly he lapped up the entire content of the bowl and settled back for a contented nap. Perhaps things were not going to be so bad after all.

<u>Woody's Story</u>

What Goes Up ...

The young Woodpecker paced up and down in his nest. He really was very hungry indeed and it seemed to have been ages since his mother had last fed him. He contented himself by practising his preening, running his beak through his, as yet, only semi-mature feathers. His emerald green wings and bright red head plumage made him look really quite handsome, he thought.

With still no sign of his mother, Woody hopped up onto the side of his nest and peered out of the hole in their tree, calling for food. For much of the day he repeated this performance and, as the late afternoon sun started to soften, he began to sense that something very bad may have happened. So, in a final desperate measure, he jumped up and perched precariously at the barky entrance of their hollow. Woody had watched his mother fly in and out of the tree hole so many times but, as yet, had not plucked up the courage to launch himself into the air because he knew his young feathers were not quite ready to support his weight.

Despite his anxious calling, which had become more and more insistent over the last few hours, there was no sign of his mother anywhere.

Even though he knew his perching techniques were not quite developed yet either, Woody chanced a little lean forwards to get a better look out of their tree. It was a decision he would soon very much regret. As he felt himself begin to topple into the great outside, instinct took over and he spread his wings. Though the effect was not dramatic, it certainly did slow his tumbled descent through the air towards the ground. Crunch! He landed, not very delicately, on the woodland floor, which was actually, to his considerable relief, quite soft and springy.

Woody was in shock. More than that though, he was afraid. How was he to regain the safety of his home in the tree, now way above his head? He huddled up to the side of the trunk, making plaintive little calls to attract his mother's attention. Still nothing. He tried his wings but there was not nearly enough power in his nestling-soft feathers to launch himself upwards to home. And he was so hungry; he didn't know what to do for the best. It was not long before he heard a noise in the distance. As it got louder, so he hoped against hope that the familiar flash of green flight feathers that were his mother's would come into view, in accompaniment of his long-lost breakfast, lunch and supper, all in one.

Far from it though: the noise was in fact a Two Legs, who was walking through the woodland. Woody, too young to know any particular fear of these creatures, bustled forward, optimistically imagining that some food might appear. Instead, the enormous Two Legs bent down and, before Woody had time to realise his mistake, firmly but gently picked him up.

"I want my Mum!" he squawked, somewhat indignantly.

Woody found himself wrapped up in a large piece of soft material, which, although not hurting, rather curtailed his struggling movements, and with still not a morsel to lay his beak to.

Over the few hours that followed, the young woodpecker experienced so many new events that he became utterly bemused. There was his journey back through the woods, a trip in a Lightning Thunder and a very odd wing-stretching, leg pulling examination by Two Legs to round it all off. Only then was he given to another Two Legs, who carried him to a strange new place, where there were many other creatures all around.

No sooner was he put inside his new home, than he reprised his desperate, hunger-fuelled cries for food. This time, finally, with resounding success. Enormous heaps of food were handed to him by Two Legs, which he gulped down with great enthusiasm. So much so, that it wasn't until his beak failed to open (for his eighth mouthful) and his small

tummy was bulging to bursting, that his eyelids half closed in contentment and he fluffed himself out before settling down for a well-earned nap. Just before the Two Legs left, they smeared some food into the bark of the tree nest that they had built for Woody; "most strange", he thought, as he tucked his head under his wing and fell fast asleep.

Upon waking, a short while later, Woody was staggered to find that he was hungry again, but, despite his calling, no food appeared. He gave the food still stuck in the bark a sideways look. Being only a youngster, Woody was used to having his food brought to him, so he wasn't entirely sure what to do about the bark-dwelling kind. Just as he was trying to decide, he heard a voice from nearby telling him to take the food if he was hungry. Pleased that his silent query had been answered, he opened his beak and waited expectantly – nothing!

"It won't come to you," said the voice "you must go to it; use your beak to peck it from between the bark."

Woody hopped forward and stabbed his beak against the bark. When he withdrew, he found a small amount of food stuck to the end of it, which he immediately gobbled down. At each stab, so a little more food came away and was greedily consumed. "This is hard work," he thought, but, sure enough, Woody had begun to learn to feed himself, as he would have to do when he returned to the wild.

Over the coming weeks, prior to his release, the sound of Woody's beak hammering repetitively and determinedly into his food supply became an extremely regular feature of life in the shed, and, though he knew it was sometimes very irritating to the other inmates, One-Eye was proud of the youngster. His instinct for survival was strong; he was learning quickly and preparing himself well for his future life.

Old Prickle's Story

A Prickly Problem

Old Prickle had lived for a great many seasons and was a very knowledgeable beast. Any of his children and, indeed, grandchildren and great grandchildren who sought his advice would always be sent on their way with a sound and sensible answer to their frequent and varied questions.

Foraging around in the autumn leaves one morning, Old Prickle was becoming increasingly concerned that food was getting harder and harder to find. Was it just a case of his failing eyesight? The loss of his acute sense of smell, perhaps? Hmm. Even with the further unhelpfulness that each passing year brought his senses, still he was convinced that there was actually less food to be found.

It seemed to Old Prickle that with every season he had known, so another piece of his favourite habitat had been taken. He was well aware that his hunting ground was becoming smaller; his world constantly disappearing before his failing eyes. Large impenetrable walls had enclosed many of his old haunts; short grass replaced the old long-overgrown areas; trees vanished; hills and dales became level and, now, as his tired old legs trundled him forward, he felt sad for the future generations, who would find life much harder than he had known in his youth.

Old Prickle, in his wisdom, had learned to become wary of any item which smelt of Two Legs. Although he had never known them do him any direct harm, he instinctively avoided contact with them, if possible. It was their discarded rubbish, after all, which littered the once clean, sweet-smelling pastures of his hoglet-hood. Plastic bags, sharp, jagged pieces of old bottles, tins, pieces of wire, were now all too frequent obstacles to be avoided.

As he rummaged deeper into the undergrowth, Old Prickle became aware of the nearby presence of young Two Legs. Before he even had time to make himself scarce, suddenly, with a great 'whoosh!', he was hit in the side by a large leather ball! As he tumbled across the leafy ground, badly winded, he saw the ball come to rest just a short distance away from where he now lay, hurt and dazed.

Almost immediately, the pounding sound of running Two Legs' feet grew close, so, despite his pain, Old Prickle reflexively managed to curl himself up into a tight, prickly ball to avoid any further injury.

He listened as the Two Legs searched for the missile which had bowled him over. He waited, totally motionless, for the comfort of silence to return. The noise, however, did not abate but, instead, grew louder, closer. Without warning, Old Prickle felt himself being rolled over none too gently. He remained curled tight but once again, and more forcibly this time, his poor old weary body was sent hurtling across the ground.

When he came to a stop, his body battered and shaking, Old Prickle tried desperately to suck in some air through his bruised lungs, before the pain struck again. And so it did. The Two Legs were using him as their new ball.

The old hedgehog's agony became so acute that he could no longer maintain his protective curled position. He felt a trickle of blood run down his nostril where his nose had been kicked, tasted its dull acid tang in the pit of his stomach. Just as the pain threatened to take him entirely, and he thought he could stand no more, a sharp angry shout from nearby sent the young Two Legs scurrying away into the distance.

Old Prickle didn't know what to think, moments later, as a single Two Legs approached, scooping soft hands under his body and gently picking him up. Prickle gave a great big shudder. Lacking the strength to curl up, he knew he was perilously exposed to many dangers, but something in the way this Two Legs handled him dispelled some of his fear. He ached terribly all over, from nose to tail and was beginning to think, with every breath he struggled to take, that the next could be his last.

Instead of being put back on the ground, Prickle felt himself being carried away. His pain became unbearable and he lapsed into unconsciousness.

When he awoke, it was to find himself lying on a hard surface, being closely examined by Two Legs. The smell of his own blood, which covered his face, filled his nostrils and there was a constant hammering noise in his ears. Prickle's old body was so bruised and swollen that even breathing proved the most tremendous effort, manageable only in slow but deep shuddering gasps, each one sending unbearable pain ripping right through him.

The Two legs carefully wiped a foul-smelling liquid over his face, nose and ears. As they did so, Prickle noticed the strangest thing; the world had become totally silent. Had he been able to look around, he would have seen the thin trickles of blood coming not only from his nose, but from his ears too. The old hedgehog lay perfectly still throughout his examination, with neither the strength nor the will to resist. Each of his legs was manipulated back and forth – though they ached insufferably, he could tell that there were no breaks, yet still, he was grateful for the Two Legs' attention to detail.

Another short, sharp pain followed, which surprised him somewhat, for he was not expecting cruelty from these Two Legs. But blessedly, soon after, a sense of tranquillity seemed to surround him and the pain floated blissfully away from his body. With the agony over, Old Prickle was soon overcome by sleep, which he knew to be one of life's greatest healers. Yes, sleep would help.

The Silent World

Old Prickle awoke gradually from his slumber with, for several wonderful seconds, absolutely no recollection whatsoever of his ordeal. However, as he became fully aware, he felt the dull ache reclaim his body. He opened his eyes slowly, wondering what to expect from the unfamiliar smelling surroundings he now found himself in. As he looked around with his failing eyesight (which had never been very good, even in his youth) he could see only that he was in a small, box-like enclosure, carpeted with newspaper. There were two bowls not that far from him, but it was not until he dragged his aching body forward, that he could scent the food piled high in one of them and the liquid in the other. Usually, as he moved around, he was aware of the sound of rustling leaves and twigs beneath his belly and the various movements and calls of the many creatures with whom he shared the outside, but today all was silent.

Tentatively, Prickle crawled towards the first bowl. He had smelt this kind of food before in old discarded cans which lay scattered around his former hunting grounds, but had always resisted the temptation to crawl into such small, confined spaces for fear of becoming trapped. He had once seen a young hog completely wedged in such an object, with only its back legs left to view; it was not until a friendly Two Legs passed by that the hog had been released from his temporary prison. Thankfully, the Two Legs had picked up the can and taken it away.

This time though, as there was no can and no other sign of danger, Old Prickle slowly licked at the food, savouring each wonderful taste. With his jaw still sore and bruised, he only managed a little of the meal before moving on to the other bowl, the contents of which looked just like water. A plentiful substance in the woodlands, found welled in the hollows of tree roots or trickling along the many ditches that ran through his homeland, Prickle remembered the times, in his younger days, when water always tasted so sweet and clean. But, as the years had passed, so the water had seemed to develop a very unpleasant 'bite' to it – sometimes metallic, sometimes bitter and, at other times, it was even cloudy or frothy. Recently, in fact, there'd been several occasions when he'd felt it wise to leave well alone and seek another source to quench his thirst elsewhere.

As Prickle lowered his great long tongue into the bowl, he was delighted to find that this water tasted not only sweet – as it used to in the old days – but sweeter still than he could ever remember it tasting. He lapped eagerly at this delicious mixture and even as he did so, he felt the goodness it provided flood through him. With his appetite and thirst temporarily satisfied, he crept back into a dark corner of his box and slept again, this time a more natural and dream-filled sleep.

Old Prickle did not wake until he was suddenly touched by a Two Legs, which caused him to panic and snap into as tight a ball as his pained body would allow. He was more worried that he had not heard the Two Legs approach, than by the Two Legs itself; *never* before had he failed to hear the nearby movement of a possible predator. But, as no further harm seemed to be forthcoming, Prickle grew curious as to what the Two Legs may be doing and eased his little black snout from his underbelly to see what was going on.

Still partly curled, Prickle saw the newspaper being removed from his cage and a new supply being carefully laid in its place, his depleted bowls of food and liquid were both replenished with heavenly smelling, fresh treats, and, as he risked watching a little while longer, the Two Legs' hand came towards him. Slipping gently under his chin, preventing him from his curling up again, he felt the hand ease some liquid into his ears. Expecting pain to follow, he was surprised when it was a more soothing sensation which trickled slowly into his head. Prickle was then returned to his box, from where he watched as the Two Legs departed.

As he was now wide-awake, he decided to venture out a bit further to see if there was any other sign of life around him.

Nearing the edge of his box, he looked out across what appeared to be a wooden building of some sort and, once he had managed to focus his eyes to the greater distance, saw other animals and birds in similar enclosures. He saw them moving, which surely must have created noise – but yet, he heard nothing. Old Prickle called out and was astounded when everyone turned to face him. This was getting stranger and stranger, he thought. The mouths and beaks of his neighbours seemed to be moving now, but still there was no sound – even his own voice had felt like more of a rumble within him than an actual noise when he'd called out just moments before. Prickle felt alone, trapped in a world which was not only alien to him, but also to his senses. Was he never to hear the majestic myriad of nature's orchestra again? Old Prickle felt very old indeed, and, all of a sudden, so very tired of life.

During the day, the Two Legs came and went several times and if he was not looking directly at them as they approached, he was taken completely unawares. Each time more drops were squeezed into his ears and each time he felt the same soothing sensation – but all this to an accompaniment of resounding silence. Although he munched on occasional morsels of food and drank plenty of pure, sweet water, it was far more by habit than desire. He already missed the sounds of the world and found it hard to envisage living without the same everyday noises that had seemed so insignificant to him in the past.

After yet another short nap, he ventured forward once more, to watch the others from the confines of his mute enclosure. Looking to the left, Prickle's gaze immediately fell upon an owl who, using his wing as a form of a pointer, seemed to be desperately gesturing to Old Prickle to look across the building at a large cage on the other side. Old Prickle turned in the direction of the owl's notion only to find a young-looking fox staring at him intently. Old Prickle sensed that the fox had something to show him and nodded his head to confirm he was paying attention.

With that, the fox bent down and clamped his large feeding bowl firmly between his jaws. Prickle looked on in bewildered amazement as the fox, obviously planning to send the bowl crashing across the front of his cage with as much force as he could muster, threw his head to one side in preparation to let rip! Prickle wondered what on earth all this could possibly be in aid of. *Crash!* went the bowl, as it flew out of the fox's mouth and hurtled into the metal of the cage door. Old Prickle moved back, startled. Had he actually heard the crashing noise, or just seen and felt it? As the fox got set to repeat his action, Prickle closed his eyes in order to concentrate fully on what would happen next. After a few moments, he definitely heard a muffled sound and opened his eyes to see if the bowl had been thrown, which, indeed, it had. Prickle laughed in sheer delight. So that was what they had been up to! His fellow creatures had been trying to prove to him that he could in fact hear a little and that his deafness would very possibly not be permanent. He turned, now, to the owl who, though once again perched quietly on his branch, had a very large smile on his face.

Sure enough, over the weeks that followed, Prickle slowly began to hear just a little more as each day passed. The drops, which were still being put in his ears, helped to ease whatever blockage remained and, as his hearing began to return, surprisingly enough, so did his appetite for food and for life.

Over time, Prickle's hearing healed enough that he was able to converse with the other inhabitants of the shed and even partake in the odd sing-song. The youngsters loved his old woodland folk songs and often had him, in his rich, gravelly voice, chorusing melodies way into the darkened hours. Through One-Eye's wisdom and the many other accompanying stories of reassurance from the others, Prickle knew that all would be well and that, when ready, he would be returned to his homeland.

Old Prickle didn't feel quite so old any more.

Magpie's Story

The Entwining Prison

Magpie stood, woebegone, on the riverbank. Supported mainly by a large tuft of grass, his weakened body trembled in the cold of the early morning frost. For three days he had been shackled by a large, tangled mass of fishing line, which, biting cruelly into both feet, was causing him a great deal of pain. Even with all his feathers puffed out to their maximum capacity, the freezing wind was beginning to slow his reactions considerably.

Today was traditionally the day when all creatures of air and land met together in as large a group as possible, to tell their tales and give thanks to the Great Tree Owl, who, as their old lore said, came to protect them from all bad things. But, as Magpie looked down at his sore, bound feet, he knew he was going nowhere. The weather had been much wilder three days ago when Magpie, who prided himself on his hunting skills, had decided to venture away from his usual feeding ground in search of some extra food. He was in superb condition, his sleek black wings and snow-white belly shining in the watery sun. Since childhood, Magpie had meticulously heeded his mother's teachings and preened himself thoroughly after every meal. This served not only to maintain his handsome appearance but, more importantly, to protect his feathers from the wet and damp. When roosting in the rain, he would watch as the droplets of water ran smoothly from his back, one sharp shake after such rain would dispel any remaining drops and leave him free to soar into the sky with supreme manoeuvrability.

As he flew over a small wooded area, he came to a river which meandered quietly through large, flat pastureland. That would be a great place to pick up some tasty morsels, he thought, minutely altering the angle of his wings in order to glide lower towards the riverbank. On closer inspection, the fertile land beside the water did indeed seem to be an ideal place to have a special meal, so he wheeled round and landed gently on a low bush. He hopped to the ground and made an early start on his forage for breakfast.

Magpie's new feeding ground did not disappoint him. In a very short time, his belly was rounded and full. Though he knew it was a little greedy of him, he strutted through the grass for one final mouthful. Suddenly, he staggered

forward, his feet seemingly stuck in a piece of matted grass. In shuffling backwards to free himself, he found that he was more entwined than he'd first thought and bent down to release his trapped feet using his strong, sharp beak. The knot wasn't one of grass, however, but an impenetrable nylon line. Not unduly worried, Magpie started to tug and pull at the mass, expecting it to come loose, but the more he struggled, the more firmly he became anchored and, slowly, with panic creeping up over him, his stabbing attacks at the nylon grew anxious and frantic. Soon the sides of his beak bled from his frenzied effort and his feet were throbbing painfully as the nylon bit deeper and deeper into his skin. After a long while, he finally slumped down exhausted and frightened.

During the course of the next day, Magpie made several unsuccessful attempts to break free; each effort only causing the nylon to dig deeper into his flesh, until his feet were cut so badly he could no longer stand. Magpie had no choice that night, but to lay, barely hidden, in the low grasses, where he hoped desperately to remain unseen by any would-be enemies. He slept lightly, each minute noise immediately alerting his senses.

As dawn approached, the scent of a fox had him wide-eyed and listening intently. Magpie could barely breathe as he heard the crunch of the animal's paws on the frost-crisp grass, approach his hiding place. He gave one almighty wrench with his feet to try and flee from his foe. Not only was he still stuck fast, but in his panic he managed to twist awkwardly and heard the sickly snap of his leg, as he tumbled over. The pain, although not as great as he might have expected, rendered his leg useless, so he was forced to right himself, using his wings as support. Now weak from all his exertion over the last couple of days, frightened and in great pain, he peered through the morning mist, only to see the fox ambling off into the distance. Luckily, he had been down wind from the predator, who had probably finished hunting for the night anyway.

The next day passed as before, but, fortunately, no likely natural enemies troubled him. Rather, his prime concerns remained: the cold, his growing hunger and the throbbing pain which now crept cruelly up his legs and into his body.

Magpie settled back to meet the Great Tree Owl, he knew it would not be long now. Another heavy darkness fell and when night eventually turned to morning, with no energy left, he slid down on his haunches with his head tucked under his wing, waiting for his final journey to begin.

Even when a huge Two Legs loomed large above him, still, he did not possess the strength to move. The Two Legs' stooped down and cradled Magpie's trembling body and Magpie readied himself to meet his fate.

When the nylon mass did not shift, the Two Legs produced a long, thin, shiny stick which severed the tangled knot from the ground. Magpie felt himself being lifted up, free at last from the damp ground, and gently tucked inside the Two Legs' soft coat. Relieved to be out of the cold, but with no hope, Magpie closed his eyes, his aching body now being warmed by the closeness of the strange body against which he rested.

Footloose

Magpie's journey seemed endless. He was beginning to get most frustrated that he could not just be left to travel toward the Great Tree Owl in peace. Instead, he was being kept awake as, with the comfort of warmth, the throbbing ache in his legs and feet was slowly becoming much, much worse. He began to struggle in his dark cocoon. As unfriendly as it had seemed at the time, he realised, the numbing cold of the outside world had served to numb a lot of the pain in his entangled feet.

Still weak with hunger, his fidgeting protest did not last long and he did his best to settle himself down once again, not knowing where he was being taken, or how much longer he would be a stowaway in the Two Legs' coat. After much time, during which he had been aware of many strange sounds and movements, Magpie felt the same gentle hand surround him, withdrawing him from his dark shelter and taking him into a new, unfamiliar environment. He could no longer see grass or sky, but a place with many peculiar objects all around and several small suns shining down upon him. There were other Two Legs standing close by and before he knew it one of them had taken him gently but firmly in hand. Encasing his wings to prevent him from flying, the Two Legs made odd but quietly soothing noises to him, whilst thoroughly examining his legs and feet.

Magpie, being both tired and scared, twisted his neck this way and that, trying to find a means of escape. His strong black beak snapped at any object that came too close, though the way in which he was being held prevented him from inflicting any serious damage. As the inspection of his legs and feet continued, he gradually came to realise that the remaining nylon bonds were being released from his feet with the help of an odd, shiny beak that was continually snip-snip-snipping at any exposed ends. In addition to this, his sore toes were being regularly dampened with a nasty-smelling liquid which, although stung at first, after a few seconds seemed to dull the agonising pain he'd suffered without reprieve for the last few days.

Out of the corner of his panic-widened eye, Magpie saw a finger within grabbing distance. Darting forward, he clamped the offending digit firmly in his strong, sharp beak. Magpie was quite put out by the lack of effect his attack seemed to have. He was not, as he had hoped to be, immediately released; instead there came only a small strangled sound from one of the Two Legs, as the other moved forward to prize his beak gently apart and release the finger.

Having been distracted by his escape attempts, when Magpie finally did look down to his feet it was to see that they were entirely free of every last piece of their former nylon imprisonment. Though he was extremely pleased at this, the sight of his incredibly swollen and disfigured toes startled him; he still had very little feeling in his legs at all. Magpie comforted himself with the thought that at least he might now be left alone quietly, to heal. But instead he felt his body being turned over and his broken leg explored.

Very gently the Two Leg's hand pulled at his crooked limb, until it was once again straight, set at the right angle. Carefully, a hard, strong substance was wrapped over nearly his entire leg, from his thigh to his knee, preventing him from moving it at all. How, thought Magpie, would he possibly be able to walk around and search for food?

The stress and anxiety of the past few days begun to catch up with Magpie, making his eyelids droop in sheer exhaustion. So, when he was eventually placed into a warm, dimly lit enclosure, he settled back, convinced that, surely, this time, he would at last be embarking on his final journey.

A special perch-cum-nest had been prepared which enabled him to rest without falling over, and, looking around his new home, he noticed that both tempting morsels of food and a bowl of fresh clean water had been placed within easy pecking distance for him. Only now did he, slowly, start to become aware of familiar sounds all around him and, as the Two Legs left, so the noise increased until he heard a booming "Ssshhh!" from what he knew to be an owl.

Magpie shuffled himself round in order to locate the source of the voice and saw, perched a little way away, a magnificent golden brown Tawny Owl.

As the owl opened his beak to speak to again, Magpie couldn't help but notice that the owl was not looking directly towards him, but seemed to be gazing far into the distance, as if at some hidden sight.

"Well," said One-Eye "how do you feel? We heard of your arrival and have been waiting all day for you to come to us."

Magpie was mesmerised by One-Eye's soothing tone and the glorious feeling of calm that flooded over him as the majestic bird spoke. It was a while before he answered. "Where am I?" he said, as was the first questioned asked by so many of the shed's new arrivals.

"You're safe and will be well cared for," said Owl, resolutely.

"But I can't escape, I can barely move!" replied Magpie, who was still staring directly at the unblinking owl.

"Do not fear," said One-Eye, "just as soon as the time comes when you are able to return home to your own hunting grounds, I can promise you that this will indeed happen. For now, eat and drink first and then rest. You will be fine."

Magpie felt hypnotised. With no more questions coming to mind, he found himself taking some of the delicious, long-overdue food and drink, before settling down to rest his weary body.

Simon's Message

For as long as I can remember, I have been motivated by a deep desire to help and protect the natural world. It is difficult to pinpoint exactly where this emotional feeling comes from, but suffice it to say that it has guided me through the years in almost everything I have done. To be able to help living, sentient creatures; to offer them care and peace, and veterinary assistance – and to return them again to the wild when healed of their wounds and free from all distress – this has been the greatest reward and privilege of my life.

And it is, I believe, more rewarding and right in itself than practically any other pursuit, or calling – simply because animals, unlike the downtrodden or forgotten of the human world, have nobody to speak for them. Until now. This 'call of the wild' and a desire to find empathy with animals is all I have ever wanted to do, and for the first time, I feel that I have been able to bring something of this mysterious link with animals to life – to be able to express, in the form of a creative work, what animals *might* be thinking. In the adventures of the creatures within this book, I have attempted to show an animal's suffering and sense of dislocation, and to make readers understand – I hope – how our actions as human beings often have appalling consequences.

In our materialistic lives – existences that are conducted at ever-increasing speeds, and which are increasingly separate from the natural world – the environment and its delicate tapestry of wildlife are forgotten. Indeed, 'environment' – 'wildlife' have almost become just vague, background words which we hear on the television, as we surf and surge through our distracted and careless world. The countryside flashes past us from our car windows, but how often do we stand and stare, and take in – and *understand* the world around us?

Wildlife Aid has fought for some 30 years for the animal kingdom and the countryside which is our common heritage. Without the modest, Surrey farmhouse hospital which we founded and worked so hard to build up – an organisation staffed almost entirely by volunteers, and maintained by endless fundraising and generosity – so many animals would have simply been left to die from their injuries or from neglect. And without the countless talks and lectures which we have given to schools, colleges and community groups, many hundreds of people might have gone through life without that all-important appreciation of the world with which we humans co-exist.

As this book of animal tales goes to press, we at Wildlife Aid are working day after day to bring to life another great dream: a planned, permanent visitors' centre and educational facility, hospital and wildlife centre all rolled into one. Our vision is, that one day, the United Kingdom will have – here in rural, greenbelt Surrey – a true centre for conservation, learning and environmental and wildlife protection. If you have enjoyed the animal tales in this book, and feel that you would like to lend a hand – either as a volunteer, donor, subscriber, supporter, fundraiser, patron, educator, mentor, worker, ambassador, communicator, leaflet distributor or general helper – we would love to hear from you.

Books should be able to open minds, and we hope that this little volume will also be able to open doors – a door through which we can learn to love wildlife, a door to a new centre for British and international conservation. Together, I feel certain that we can build a secure and viable future for British wildlife, and for the landscapes, too, which make natural freedom possible, and which provide so much spiritual refreshment for our tired modern minds and bodies.

Simon Cowell

Help us to help Britain's wildlife!

If you have been stirred by the story of One-Eye and inspired by the work of Wildlife Aid, we invite you to write a new chapter of our story! On this detachable form, you can register your support for our work. And you can do this in a variety of ways.

Firstly, in the space just below, give us your name, address, telephone number, or email if you would like to join our mailing list or become a member – or, better still, an active volunteer! Voluntary work can take many forms at Wildlife Aid – from helping day-to-day at our site – to taking the initiative in your community as a fundraiser – to talking about our work to schools and community groups.

....

....

....

Or thirdly, tick this box ☐ if you would like to make your own donation to our work, or to leave a legacy.

I/we enclose a donation of £…....… to Wildlife Aid.

All you now need to do is to tear this page from the book and send it to us at:

Wildlife Aid, Randalls Farmhouse, Randalls Road, Leatherhead, Surrey, KT22 OAL.

Or visit our website and complete your details online – **www.wildlifeaid.org.uk**

Registered Charity No. 297610

Simon Cowell MBE *was once a commodity broker. Yet the world of London, commuting and international finance offered only a limited horizon. Beating in Simon's heart throughout his life was a desire to protect our wildlife and the wild places upon which our very ecology and environmental survival depend. So he decided to put his suit and briefcase away – for good – and dedicate his life to the creation, not just of a wildlife*

hospital which would simply react to the sufferings and injury which animals have to endure, but to build an organisation which would educate, speak out and campaign to change hearts and minds.

Little could Simon have foreseen how his modest early idea for a wildlife centre would develop. Today, Wildlife Aid features in its own long-running television series – something which has given Simon's work a level of exposure and popularity of which most charities could only dream. Now, he has set out on his greatest project to date – the creation of a British centre for animal conservancy and education.

www.wildlifeaid.org.uk
www.simon-cowell.org.uk

Jo Maynard *began drawing as soon as she could hold a crayon, and as a child loved to create pictures of domestic pets and wildlife. With a reputation for fine pet and wildlife portrait drawings, Jo's compelling and splendid artwork was the natural choice for the*

story of One-Eye. Jo took up the Olympic sport of fencing at the age of ten – she competed in over 50 international tournaments as part of the British team, and having been British number one for two years, retired in order to pursue her artwork.

www.artbyjomaynard.co.uk